The Terrible, Horrible, Very Bad Good News

MEGHNA PANT

EBURY PRESS
An imprint of Penguin Random House

EBURY PRESS

USA | Canada | UK | Ireland | Australia
New Zealand | India | South Africa | China

Ebury Press is part of the Penguin Random House group of companies whose addresses can be found at global.penguinrandomhouse.com

Published by Penguin Random House India Pvt. Ltd
7th Floor, Infinity Tower C, DLF Cyber City,
Gurgaon 122 002, Haryana, India

Penguin Random House India

First published in Ebury Press by Penguin Random House India 2021

10 9 8 7 6 5 4 3 2 1

This is a work of fiction. Names, characters, places and incidents are either the product of the author's imagination or are used fictitiously and any resemblance to any actual person, living or dead, events or locales is entirely coincidental.

ISBN 9780143453543
Typeset in Adobe Caslon Pro by Manipal Technologies Limited, Manipal
Printed at Replika Press Pvt. Ltd, India

www.penguin.co.in

FSC
www.fsc.org
MIX
Paper from responsible sources
FSC® C016779

EBURY PRESS

THE TERRIBLE, HORRIBLE, VERY BAD GOOD NEWS

Meghna Pant is a multiple award-winning author, journalist, feminist and speaker.

Her books—*How to Get Published in India*, *Feminist Rani*, *The Trouble with Women*, *Happy Birthday* and *One & a Half Wife*—have been published to commercial and critical acclaim.

Pant has been felicitated with various honours and her works have been shortlisted for distinguished contribution to literature, gender issues and journalism, including the Bharat Nirman Award, Laadli Media Award, FICCI Young Achiever's Award, The Lifestyle Journalist Women Achievers' Award, FON South Asia Short Story Award, Muse India Young Writer Award, Amazon Breakthrough Novel Award, Frank O'Connor International Award and the Commonwealth Short Story Prize.

Pant has been invited as a speaker for the nation's biggest literary festivals and conferences, and has appeared as a panellist on prime-time news and international channels to discuss gender issues. Pant has written articles for and been quoted in leading national and international media.

She has worked as a business news anchor for Times Now, NDTV and Bloomberg-UTV in New York and Mumbai.

She currently lives in Mumbai with her husband and two daughters.

To women everywhere—
you're more than a walking womb

1

'Congratulations,' the doctor says. 'She's pregnant.'

'What?' Mrs Joshi exclaims in utter shock. She turns to give her daughter Ladoo an incredulous look. 'How can she be pregnant? She's not even married!'

Ladoo adjusts her dupatta and looks at her mother sheepishly.

'Maa. I—' she begins.

'You keep quiet, Ladoo,' Mrs Joshi says, really angry now. 'I had told you to not let those dogs into our house! But you! You never listen to me. What will people say now?'

'Maa, I'll find a way out!' Ladoo says. 'I promise.'

She turns to the doctor and asks, 'Dr Ma'am, what are the options for an unplanned pregnancy?'

'Well,' the doctor says slowly, 'there's always the option to terminate.'

The doctor gets up and takes out an injection from a cupboard drawer.

Ladoo stares at the injection, horrified. Mrs Joshi indicates to the doctor to keep the injection away.

'Sorry, Dr Ma'am,' Mrs Joshi says. 'Ladoo is scared of injections. Only her father can handle her around them.'

The doctor nods and quickly puts the injection away.

Ladoo looks relieved. She lifts her pet dog Billi from the floor, and asks the doctor, 'Dr Ma'am, will it not be better to let Billi keep the pregnancy? After all, dogs make the best single mothers, don't they?'

'*Dhat*,' her mother says, as she raps Ladoo on the head.

Ladoo averts her gaze to the doctor's table, where there's a desk nameplate which reads:

ANUBHA NEGI, ANIMAL VET

*

They walk back home with Billi, to the Income Tax Colony, Swarg Lok, where they live. Ladoo's father, Mr Deepak Joshi, is an income tax commissioner. Their colony is near Rishikesh's famous Lakshman Jhula, a suspension bridge, and contains a row of small townhouses, all yellow and brown in colour, all laid out in a row, where everyone has lived together for decades.

Mrs Joshi and Ladoo cross the Lakshman Jhula, which, according to Ladoo, is the finest point to marvel at her beautiful hometown, Rishikesh. She takes a moment to admire it: the Ganga; the Himalayas; the ghats; the temple bells ringing; devotees chanting; *aarti*s with dancing flames; the graffiti of Shiva; sadhus, dressed as Lord Hanuman, practising yoga; a white tourist feeding a cow.

Mrs Joshi is still sulking. Ladoo hugs her mother. She mouths a sorry. Mrs Joshi relents and smiles at her older daughter. She pets Billi and pats her bulging stomach.

Then, Mrs Joshi goes about her morning routine. She stops to pluck marigolds from a bush. She offers these at a Shiv–Parvati temple. She stops to buy fruits and vegetables from a vendor. She snaps the end of a bhindi to check if it's firm enough. She taps a watermelon to check if it's ripe. She puts these in Ladoo's cloth bag. She haggles with a chaat-wallah and buys shakarkandi for her husband. She puts these in Ladoo's bag as well.

Ladoo enters a small shop in the market and comes out with a dozen eggs, hidden under her dupatta. Mrs Joshi eyes them with distaste and sprays *gangajal* on them. Ladoo quickly puts these in a separate cloth bag she's carrying.

Ladoo carries the bulging bags uncomfortably, while trying to control Billi, as Mrs Joshi stops to greet someone. Fortunately, after ten minutes, they reach Swarg Lok.

'Jai Bholenath,' Ladoo and her mother shout out to their neighbours, in unison.

Ladoo likes her life and her set-up, even though her younger sister Tamara and she are considered the black sheep of the town. Ladoo is divorced and childless. Tamara is a social media influencer—under the handle 'Hot Yogini'—who always wears revealing yoga clothes. Ladoo doesn't mind that her neighbours are interfering, narrow-minded or judgemental, because they're also friendly and loyal.

On reaching home, house number 111, Ladoo immediately gets to work. She gives Billi food, sets the eggs to boil and opens up the bags. She hugs Mina Bua, her father's unmarried sister, who lives with them, and whom she's close to. Then she goes up to the terrace of their little town house, carrying a plate of boiled eggs.

Ladoo looks around to check if anyone's watching. She walks over to a cot, where mirchi is laid out for drying, unzips the *gadda* and takes out a pregnancy stick.

Suddenly, she hears a sound behind her. Oh no! Has she been caught? Ladoo turns around in shock. Phew! It's only Tamara; young, thin and beautiful, dressed up in shorts and a *ganji*.

'Jai Bholenath,' Ladoo tells Tamara. 'I thought it was that Kamini Kavya!'

Kavya is their bitchy neighbour, who's always interfering in the sisters' private lives.

Ladoo pats Tamara's head affectionately and hands her the plate of eggs.

'Here are your banned goods,' she says. 'One day someone will catch you, Tammy!'

Non-vegetarian food is banned in Rishikesh, but—like a typical Indian—Tamara thinks that rules are made so they can be broken.

'Who cares, Dids?' the twenty-eight-year-old Tamara says, shrugging her shoulders. She takes a bite of the egg. 'You know I only *give* tension. I never take tension.'

Ladoo grins at Tamara. She takes the pregnancy stick and sneaks into the small bathroom on the terrace.

She sits down on the pot, with the stick in her hand, and pees on it. She bites her nails in tension, waiting. Only one line appears. She breathes out, annoyed, and shakes the stick. She pees on it some more. The stick still shows only one line.

'So bloody unfair!' the thirty-four-year-old grumbles. 'How come even Billi can get pregnant, and I can't?'

Ladoo leaves the stick on the sink and comes out of the bathroom. She finds Tamara sprawled on the mirchi gadda, making a video of herself smoking a joint.

'Tammy! I told you not to hide your ganja next to my pregnancy sticks. Maybe that's the reason I'm not getting pregnant!' she scolds her sister.

'Don't be so extra, Dids,' Tamara says, using her usual millennial slang. 'And shhh! I'm making Rishikesh's best Insta video. "Hot Yogini Does Ganja". Guaranteed 10,000 views.'

'You millennials!' Ladoo says. 'You're the world's only generation that makes doing nothing look like something!'

'You know you're a millennial too, right?'

'I know. But I feel like a boomer, Tammy.'

Ladoo plops down next to Tamara. Tamara stops recording her video and looks at her sister, concerned.

'Why? What happened, Dids?' Tamara asks.

'Nothing, Tammy. I'm still *not* pregnant,' Ladoo whispers.

'You're also not . . . ' Tammy says and makes a wedding *shehnai* sound, ' . . . married.'

Ladoo sighs and adds, 'I told Ricky I was on the pill, so he wouldn't use a condom. I was ovulating that day. I even made sure he ate bananas before so . . . you know . . . his sperm count increased. Still . . . nothing.'

'Ovulate???' Tamara asks her loudly.

'Shhh! Kamini Kavya might be listening to us!' Ladoo says. She pushes the clothes on the clothesline to one side and looks around for her neighbour on the adjacent terrace. No one's there. Ladoo heaves a deep sigh of relief and continues, 'Ovulation is the only time that a woman can get pregnant, two weeks after her period.'

'You've lost it, Dids! Are you even speaking English?' Tamara says, looking seriously at Ladoo. 'Look, I'm woke and all, and I know it's 2021 and all, but are you sure you know what you're doing? What if you *actually* get pregnant?'

Ladoo looks at Tamara, confused, 'That *is* the plan!'

'The plan is to get knocked up and guilt Ricky into proposing?'

'Of course! We are Indians. Pregnancy means marriage.'

'One second, so if he proposes, you'll actually . . . for reals . . . *marry* Ricky?'

'Obvs yes,' Ladoo says, looking at her sister like she's calling the sun yellow.

'But . . . what about Mr Right?'

'Forget Mr Right. I need *Mr Right Now*.'

'Dids, no! Yuck! You cannot marry that loser. He wears a red tilak on his forehead all day! He introduces himself as, "Myself Ricky". His real name is Ratneshwaram!'

'So?' Ladoo shrugs. She gets up from the cot and begins to hang some of the wet clothes that are lying in a bucket.

'So?' Tamara says in surprise. 'You deserve better than Ricky, Dids. He's so yuck!'

'Don't say that about your future *jiju*.'

'If you actually get pregnant with his child,' Tamara says, 'you'll be better off as a single mother.'

'Being a single mother involves being single,' Ladoo says. 'And you know me, I can't be alone.'

'Fine!' Tamara says. 'Anyway, he's Garhwali and we're Kumaoni. Mom won't even allow you to marry him.'

Ladoo looks earnestly at her sister and says, 'And I've told you, Tammy, you won't understand. I'm a childless divorcee. I'm going to be thirty-five in a few months! This is my last chance to have a baby. So, I can either have an accidental pregnancy and trick the guy into marrying me, or I can freeze my eggs and keep waiting for Mr Right. And, trust me, pregnancy is the cheaper and easier option.'

'Dids, so much drama over having a child?' Tamara says. 'Why? Kids are *so* annoying!'

'Kids are annoying in your twenties . . . but a necessity in your thirties. Got it?'

'Fine, Dids, but I don't think this country needs one more kid!' Tamara says. 'We have *so* many already.'

'And I don't think me having one kid will affect our population of 1.3 billion people!' Ladoo snaps.

'Whatevs, Dids,' Tamara adds. 'Sadhguru says that women who choose to not have kids must be rewarded, and that you should find something else to involve yourself with, like yoga. That's what I do! Why don't you try that?'

'Tammy, the only thing I want to involve myself with is a baby,' Ladoo says. 'So, I can't afford to wait, ok?'

'Why not? Kareena Kapoor and Farah Khan had their babies in their forties.'

'Celebrity eggs are different, yaar. They are like Katrina Kaif. My eggs are like Shakti Kapoor. That's the problem.'

Tamara looks at the boiled eggs on her plate and pushes it towards Ladoo.

'So have my eggs, Dids,' she says innocently.

Ladoo looks at her sister and laughs.

Tamara smiles back and passes her the joint. Ladoo shakes her head.

Just then Tamara's phone buzzes. She puts down her joint, jumps up from the gadda, and shouts, 'Yes! It's Shirtless Sandy time!'

Tamara runs in excitement to the front of the terrace.

All the ladies of Swarg Lok also come running to their terrace.

They spot Sandeep Oberoi at the gate. He's in his late thirties, buffed and shirtless. He is coming back from his everyday morning run, but, to the women, he seems to be jogging in slow motion. They all sigh.

'I don't know why he's even wearing clothes,' says Tamara, annoyed. 'Milind Soman once ran nude. And they're both from Mumbai, *na*?'

Ladoo laughs, as Sandeep jogs past house number 111.

Tamara sighs blissfully and sings, '*Bombay se aaya mera dost, dost ko salaam karo.*'

Tamara waves to Sandeep and lifts Ladoo's hands and forces her to wave.

'Why don't you scramble his eggs, Dids?' she tells Ladoo.

'Shush, Tammy! That's so disgusting. He's married,' Ladoo says. Tamara giggles. Ladoo rolls her eyes and adds, 'And what kind of feminist are you anyway, Tammy? Objectifying men like this?'

'It's ok, Dids,' Tamara says, taking a slow bite of the egg. 'I'm a very *bad* feminist.'

Ladoo can't help but laugh out loud.

Suddenly, they hear Mrs Joshi's voice from downstairs, 'Tammy, your room is a mess! Come down this second and clean it!'

Tamara runs out of the terrace, shouting back sweetly, 'Coming, Mommmmmm!'

'Maa's pet,' Ladoo says sarcastically. 'I wish I was Maa's favourite child! Even I'd get to eat eggs at home.'

Ladoo hears Mrs Joshi's heavy footsteps coming up the stairs to the terrace. She suddenly remembers—'Fuck, I left my pregnancy stick in the bathroom.' She runs into the bathroom and searches for the stick. She finds it on the sink and throws it out of the window.

Just then Mrs Joshi enters the terrace. She sees Tamara's joint burning the gadda and shouts accusingly, 'Ladoooooo!'

[illegible]

Tanuja sniffs the dhal and dips. [illegible] don't [illegible]

Then [illegible] and [illegible] Ladoo's hand and [illegible] her to [illegible].

'Why don't [illegible]?' she tells Ladoo.

[illegible] Tanuja. [illegible] Ladoo [illegible] her eye and [illegible]. 'And what kind of [illegible] are you anyway? Tanuja [illegible] that?'

'[illegible],' Tanuja says, taking a few bites of the [illegible].

Ladoo can't help but [illegible] food.

Suddenly, the [illegible] for [illegible]. '[illegible] mess! Come down this instant and clean it!'

Ladoo [illegible] heading back over to [illegible].

'[illegible]' [illegible] the [illegible] of [illegible].

Ladoo hears Mrs [illegible] heavy footsteps coming up the stairs to the terrace. She [illegible] — [illegible] [illegible] the bathroom and searches for the [illegible]. She [illegible] on the tank and throws it [illegible] the window.

[illegible] Mrs [illegible] enters the terrace [illegible] Tanuja [illegible] and [illegible] Ladoo [illegible].

2

Ladoo stands outside a swanky space, called Bharosa Fertility Clinic, the only one in a row of middle-class shops and offices at the Swargashram market. She watches women go in and out. She looks at their pregnant bellies and rubs her flat one.

A man comes up behind her and makes a smooching sound. 'Tcch . . . tcch. *Ae, Chikni*.'

Ladoo turns around to slap the molester and stops. She sees 410 (Four Ten), her best friend—four feet ten inches tall, thirty-eight years old, single and dressed in a sharp suit, as always.

'Seriously, 410?' she says. 'That's not funny. You'll get beaten up one day.'

Ladoo smacks him. He grins.

'What's funny though is how late we are to office . . . again,' he tells her. 'Hurry up!'

They start walking briskly towards their office, which is in the same street.

410 points at the clinic and asks Ladoo, 'Are you ever going to go in?'

'I don't know,' says Ladoo and shrugs.

'You know you have to, right? This is the *only* place in Rishikesh where you'll find your Vicky Donor . . . '

'You can say sperm donor, idiot,' Ladoo interrupts him.

' . . . or be able to freeze your eggs. *Thanda anda*!' 410 adds, ignoring Ladoo. He laughs at his own lame joke. Ladoo rolls her eyes.

'Shhh. Talk softly,' says Ladoo. 'Somebody will hear us.'

'Don't behave like your mother!' 410 says.

He stops to help Ladoo over a little pothole in the road.

'I'll tell you what I told my friend Bobby, when he asked me, just before we went skydiving: What happens if my parachute doesn't open?' 410 says.

'What happens?' Ladoo asks.

'You jump to a conclusion,' says 410 and chuckles. Alone.

He looks at Ladoo, concerned.

'Let me guess,' he says. 'Knowing you, you are worried that if you have a baby using Vicky Donor, then you won't find true love? Your Mr Right?'

'I said keep quiet, 410!' Ladoo says. 'Someone will hear you!'

'Who cares, man?'

'Don't irritate me in the morning, 410. Mind your own business.'

'Business is all I'm minding. Insurance. Mutual funds. Bears. Bulls.'

'That no one reads.'

'They don't read your boring articles, boss, but my videos are very popular. My *Rishi Kesh to Rishi Cash* video got 1111 views. Along with 111 marriage proposals and counting, ok?'

'I know,' Ladoo says sarcastically. 'If I were thin and hot, then maybe I could also make videos that everybody would watch. Then I would also become a hero in the Gujarati community in Rishikesh. Which is—what—all of *eleven* people?'

They enter their office, Rishi Cash Times, a rundown media company with newspapers and files lining the walls. Even though the place has no buzz at all, Ladoo has been working there as a financial journalist for eleven years—her first and only job—and she loves it.

410 looks at a pretty girl, who smiles coyly at him, and says, 'That new intern . . . Shazia . . . we worked till veryyyyyyy late last night.'

'Amazing,' Ladoo says. 'Your height is only four feet ten inches, but . . . '

'A man is not known for the length of his body, but for the length of his . . . '

'Control, yaar! I've been your best friend since school, but I'm still a lady!'

'More like shady,' 410 says.

Ladoo rolls her eyes.

They reach Ladoo's desk. Someone quickly scuttles over to 410, bringing him his morning coffee.

'I wish I were the boss's son,' says Ladoo sarcastically.

'Jealous much?' asks 410.

He takes a loud sip of his coffee.

'At least share,' Ladoo says.

'It's a cappuccino. Too many calories for your permanent diet.'

Ladoo glares at him and says, 'I diet so I can remain fertile,'

410 plonks himself on Ladoo's desk and asks in a sing-song voice, '*Acha*, what happened to Ricky, with the big pricky?'

'Shhh!' Ladoo says. In a sad voice, she adds, 'Last night, on Insta, he put up a photo of himself holding dumb-bells. It was captioned: "Tell Yourself Your Hot #NoMoreBodyShaming."'

She puts down her purse and lunch *dabba*.

'I commented—innocently—that the short form of "you are" is "you're" not "your". He replied: "your a bitch . . . get you're fat ass out of here". He dumped me ya. That too on Insta. This is why I hate social media. Too many misunderstandings.'

Ricky's photo flashes across Ladoo's mind and she crosses it out.

'Another loser?' 410 says. 'You know you have a type, right?'

'Shut up.'

'*Your* a psycho magnet,' he says and laughs.

Ladoo rolls her eyes. Just then they hear a whistle. The company's HR head, Sanaya, shouts, 'As per the government health scheme, launched for every office in

Rishikesh, let's begin Tandrusti by the Minute! Everyone, take your positions.'

Ladoo and 410 line up, as the remaining eight employees form two rows. They all start doing surya namaskars, without any enthusiasm, except for 410.

'What is this stupid scheme, yaar?' Ladoo grumbles. She hates exercising. 'Totally useless.' She huffs as she tries to bend into a *padasana*. 'And I am *not* a psycho magnet. Suresh was not a psycho,' she says.

'What??? Your ex-husband? He was the worst! He was Kkkkkkkk . . . Kiran material,' 410 says. They plank to hold the *ashtanga phalakasana*. 'Have you forgotten? He was on drugs all the time! He was so high, his *thing* would not go up! Remember, I gave him Viagra on his birthday?'

Ladoo sighs, struggling to hold the asana.

410 continues, 'And, do you remember that time when he was so high, he couldn't put a plug in a socket? Twenty minutes we stared at him, while he kept trying and missing.' 410's entire body shakes with laughter. 'What fun that was! I miss that little weirdo.'

Ladoo turns to glare at 410 and falls down.

Sanaya yells, 'Once again, Ladoo is the most unfit employee in this office.'

Ladoo bangs her head against the floor. She gets up slowly.

'Ok. Ok. Sorry!' 410 tells her sweetly, still holding his plank position. 'I've been telling you from the beginning.

Forget dating these losers. You'll be better off using a strange man's jizzzzz.'

'Will you shut up? Everyone will hear you,' says Ladoo and pushes him so he falls. She leans over and whispers, 'I told you, I'd rather freeze my eggs, and wait for Mr Right.'

Ladoo walks back to her desk and takes a tablet from a medicine bottle, which says 'Folic Acid for Expecting Mothers'. She starts her computer and clicks open her article titled—'Spend on Daughter's Education, Not Wedding'—to check the number of readers. The screen says nine. She shuts her eyes and chants to herself, 'A journalist is only a journalist when they're on camera. A journalist is only a journalist when they're on camera!' She opens her eyes and sighs. She pinches her love handles. 'And I will never be on camera.'

She begins typing.

3

Later that evening, Ladoo is sitting down for dinner with her family: Mr Joshi, Mrs Joshi, Mina Bua and Tamara. They're all chatting, when her mother stops eating and looks at Ladoo, with a smile.

'Now what, Maa?' Ladoo asks apprehensively.

'That new neighbour of ours, Sandeep Oberoi? Who was transferred from Mumbai?'

'Shirtless Sandy?' asks Tamara excitedly.

Ladoo and Tamara look at each other and giggle.

'Our cook Shanta Bai told me,' continues Mrs Joshi. 'It's confirmed that his Mrs and him will get divorced. She said that his Mrs has not made him tea in the last three days.'

'Maybe they drink coffee, Mom?' Tamara says.

Ladoo whacks Tamara below the table. They laugh.

'You keep quiet, Tammy,' Mrs Joshi says. 'Tea is our tradition, not coffee. Sandeep may be from Mumbai, but he's still a sweet traditional boy. Shanta Bai told me he doesn't eat meat. He doesn't drink. He doesn't smoke. He doesn't even have a Facebook account.'

'He sounds perfect for Dids,' says Tamara sarcastically. 'But will he remain traditional after a *divorce*?'

'Of course, he will!' says Mrs Joshi. 'Men continue to be traditional even after divorce. Only women don't.'

Ladoo spits out the water she's drinking from her glass and yells, 'Maa! That is so sexist!'

'What sexist?' Her mother pauses and glares at Ladoo. 'I raised two daughters. I'm very . . . errr, very . . . what is opposite of sexist?'

They all look at each other for an answer.

'Non-partisan . . . non-heteronormative . . . intersectional . . .' says Tamara slowly.

'Speak English, Tammy,' says her mother. 'Modern. I'm very modern. Ok? All I'm trying to tell you is that there's no harm in trying. And you don't have to do a thing. I will fix it all up.'

'Maa,' says Ladoo, 'you told me I could never marry a non-Kumaoni boy. Sandeep is not even Pahadi! He's Sindhi or something.'

'A divorced woman doesn't look at a man's caste, only his availability,' snaps Mrs Joshi.

Tamara raises her eyebrows, as she tries to hold in her laughter.

'This is gold,' she says slowly. 'I wish I were live on Insta right now.'

'You keep quiet, Tammy,' says Mrs Joshi. 'We are talking real life right now.'

Ladoo sighs and says, 'But Maa, you know that after Suresh, I don't want to have another arranged marriage.

I've told you that. It's a risk to marry a stranger, and I can't take another one.'

'That's why I'm telling you to marry a divorced guy,' says Mrs Joshi. 'He'll be as insecure as you are. Like you, he will also not want another broken marriage, another failure, another scandal.'

'Thanks, Maa!' says Ladoo, offended by her mother's insinuations.

'But why is that, Bhabhi?' Mina Bua asks quickly, to take the focus off Ladoo.

'Because nowadays, in India, people forgive one divorce, but they don't forgive two divorces. That's still a taboo. So, if Ladoo marries a divorcee, he'll never leave her. He wouldn't want more *badnami*. That's why a second marriage is truly forever.'

'Padma,' Ladoo's father interrupts his wife. 'Your *modern* theories are giving me a headache. Please stop!'

'Why should I stop?' says Mrs Joshi. 'Otherwise, you are always trying to be modern, ji? Whole day you're on that sweater . . .'

'Twitter . . . not sweater,' Tamara corrects her.

'And you bought an iPhone, just to be cool . . .' Mrs Joshi continues.

'Well, Papa bought the iPhone because he thought a smartphone is a phone that's smart enough to read the encyclopaedia,' says Tamara. 'So, he's really *not* that cool.'

Ladoo and Bua laugh.

'Exactly. So, keep quiet, ji. Have a Hajmola,' Mrs Joshi tells Mr Joshi dismissively. She takes out a Hajmola tablet and puts it in her husband's mouth. 'So, Ladoo, should I take it forward with Sandeep? I think he is your best option.'

'Let her be, Bhabhi,' Bua says.

'You keep quiet, Mina!' Mrs Joshi says. 'You didn't want to get married and now you're spoiling these girls also!'

Bua blinks in surprise at this personal attack. Ladoo quickly grabs hold of Bua's hand under the table. She knows her mother has a sharp tongue.

The landline rings. They all automatically look down at their mobile phones. They then look up in confusion, as they realize that their mobiles aren't ringing.

'*What* is calling us?' Tamara asks, looking up at the ceiling, as if searching for ghosts.

'It's the landline, *beta*,' says Mrs Joshi. 'The Internet guy said I need it for our data plan to work.'

'You mean, for his cheap tricks to work,' says Mr Joshi sarcastically.

Mrs Joshi ignores him and gets up to answer the phone.

'Hello?' she says. 'Hello, Rita. I knew it was you! You're the only one I gave this number to.' She pauses. 'Oh no! Your party is cancelled? Why? I was going to make chole chawal! What????? Hello? Hello?'

Mrs Joshi looks at all of them, in a daze.

'Is everything ok, Padma?' Mr Joshi asks.

'It was Rita, my friend from my satsang class,' says Mrs Joshi slowly. 'She is pregnant!'

'Rita is pregnant? Isn't it her fiftieth birthday party tomorrow?' asks Bua.

Mrs Joshi nods in shock. 'She called to say it's cancelled, because her morning sickness gets worse in the evening.'

'Did you hang up on her when she told you the good news?' asks Tamara.

'No, the line got disconnected,' Mrs Joshi says.

'Call her back, Maa,' Ladoo says. 'Or she'll think you thought her good news was bad news.'

'Isn't it very bad good news?' says Mrs Joshi and picks up the phone receiver in a daze. Then she puts it back down. 'I don't remember her number,' she says.

'Call her from your mobile, Bhabhi,' Bua says.

'I can't believe even my fifty-year-old friends are having children,' says Mrs Joshi. She turns to Ladoo, 'I was asking you something important. You want kids right, beta? You're always talking about it. Then you'll have to get married, right?'

'Not really, Maa,' Ladoo says slowly.

'What?' asks Mrs Joshi.

'Maa, women can get pregnant without a man or marriage,' says Ladoo.

'Jai Bholenath! Don't tell me! Have you become a Lebanese?' her mother asks.

'Lesbian, Mom,' says Tamara, looking like she's enjoying the conversation. 'Not Lebanese. L.E.S.B.I.A.N.'

'Tammy, please! Not now,' says Ladoo. She turns to her mother and adds, 'I'm not gay, Maa. I'm saying that thanks to medical technology and science, women can get pregnant without a man. One option is like that Vicky Donor movie type. You make a man a donor . . . do artificial insemination . . .'

'Do what . . . irrigation?' asks Bua.

'INSEMINATION. IUI for short. That's an option if I want a child now. It's quite simple actually. You take a man's . . . you know . . . and you can get pregnant in one minute.'

'Excuse me?' says Mrs Joshi slowly. She looks disgusted.

'Wait, Maa,' says Ladoo quickly. 'There's another option. I can freeze my eggs. That way I can have children even in my forties or fifties, like lucky Rita Aunty. It's the best option for me, because then I don't have to rush into marrying a guy that you find for me. It will take the pressure off me, and off you as well.'

Her mother is appalled. 'What are you saying, Ladoo? How can you talk like this? That too in front of your father and me? Have you no shame?' she says angrily and gets up from her chair. 'Children are meant to be born naturally. With God's blessings. Not in this horrible artificial way . . . with this nonsense about donors and irrigation . . .'

' . . . insemination,' says Bua. 'IUI.'

'Whatever it is. It's against nature. Like Rita's freak pregnancy, which—trust me—she'll regret. My daughters will do things the right way. The natural way. Not in this ridiculous upside-down cheap way. We are not that desperate.'

Mrs Joshi walks out of the room in a huff.

Ladoo looks at Tamara, Bua and her father. They all look at her in sympathy. They know what it's like to bear the brunt of Mrs Joshi's anger.

Tamara bites into an aloo paratha thoughtfully, and says, in her mother's voice, 'What will you do now, my shameless Lebanese sister! The *irrigation* of a *sweater*?'

4

A few days later, Ladoo finds herself at a baby shower, where a group of around twelve to thirteen women are playing a game. They're holding diapers in their hands and guessing what kind of mithais (crushed to look like poop) have been put inside them. Amidst claps and cheers, Ladoo picks up one diaper after another and rattles off: 'Besan ki barfi! Motichoor ke ladoo! Nariyal ki mithai! Chocolate sandesh! Imli sweets!'

The women gather around Ladoo in amazement as Reshma, her school friend whose baby shower it is, gives her a packet of diapers for winning the game.

'You've won three games in a row, Ladoo,' says Reshma, patting her pregnant belly in delight. 'It's a hat-trick! And you're amazing.'

'But what will Ladoo do with all the prizes she's won?' a snide voice cuts in. 'She's not even a mother!'

It's Kavya Sharma, aka Kamini Kavya, Ladoo's next-door neighbour. She stands with her arms crossed, glaring at Ladoo, as Ladoo shifts uncomfortably on her feet.

Kavya is the most perfect person Ladoo has ever met. And she leads the most perfect life. She is married to a powerful income-tax officer, who seems to adore her, and has two well-behaved children, a boy and a girl. On top of that, she's thin, beautiful, popular and cooks really well. No one has one bad thing to say about Kavya. Even Ladoo's parents dote on her.

But, for some reason, Kavya hates Ladoo and Tamara.

'Stop it, Kavya,' Reshma says quickly. 'Come on girls, it's time to open the gifts.'

Reshma sits down on a sofa, as the guests gather around her. She opens the first gift—a suction tube—and stares at it, confused.

'What the hell is this? For which cow?' she asks, laughing.

Ladoo replies earnestly, 'This is a breast pump, Resh. Once you begin nursing, this will help you store extra breast milk. That way the baby can be fed from a bottle, and you can get some much-needed rest.'

'Ok,' says Reshma, still not looking convinced. She holds up a cloth. 'What is this? Baby *langot*?'

'No, honey. That's a swaddle,' says Ladoo. 'You'll wrap the baby in that for the first three months. It will help the baby sleep better.'

'I have to *wrap* the baby? You mean like a tandoori chicken wrap?' Reshma asks.

'I . . . I guess so,' says Ladoo slowly. 'Just don't put mango chutney on him.'

She laughs weakly.

Reshma looks at her and says, 'But why won't the baby sleep? I thought there was a reason why people say, "I slept like a baby." I thought babies sleep for at least fourteen to sixteen hours a day!'

Everyone in the party gasps.

Reshma looks around and says, 'Jai Bholenath! I'm going to be a terrible mother.'

'Every expectant mother feels that way,' says Kavya gently. 'I know I did. Trust me. It's tough being a first-time mother, but you'll figure it out. And, it's going to be amazing.'

Ladoo looks at Kavya amazed. How is she so nice to everyone else?

'Okay,' says Reshma. She takes a deep breath. 'Yes, I will be okay. Because I have all of you! Thanks, Kavya.'

She hugs Kavya and beams at everyone. Then she opens a few more gifts—a teether, a rai pillow, mittens, a changing mat, an organic kala tikka stick, a bassinet—and holds them up to ask their purpose. Every time Ladoo knows.

'Ladoo, you are ready to be a mother way more than I am,' says Reshma, gushing in admiration.

'Well, I have read every book and article on pregnancy,' Ladoo says, smiling.

'But I've heard that once you cross thirty-five, there's no chance of becoming a mother,' says Kavya curtly. She turns to Ladoo. 'How old are you? Thirty-eighty–thirty-nine?'

Ladoo gulps. She doesn't want to answer but notices that everyone is staring at her. She slowly says, 'I am thirty-four.'

'Really? I'm thirty, and I thought you were at least ten years older than me,' says Kavya.

Ladoo cringes.

'And you're a *divorcee*?' Kavya asks, emphasizing divorcee like it's a bad word.

Ladoo gulps. Everyone is staring at her. She clutches the diaper packet she's won and nods.

'Anyway!' Kavya continues. 'Since you're still single at . . . what, thirty-four . . . even if you find a guy, it'll take at least two years for him to propose. After all, it's not like you're some beauty queen or something. Then, six months to plan the wedding, one year to settle down with the in-laws, maid, house, honeymoon, etc. After all that, you'll start trying for a baby. By that time, you'll be forty. It'll be impossible to get pregnant! Any smart man . . . or woman knows this. Which means you'll not even be able to find a man to have a baby with! No man, no baby. So . . . it's too late for you, babe. Sorry. It looks like your train has left the station.'

'Kavya!' Reshma says, shocked by how mean her friend is being to Ladoo. She gets up and holds Ladoo's hand.

'What, Resh?' says Kavya defensively. 'Why should I lie to Ladoo when everyone knows the truth? Why give her false hopes?'

Ladoo's face falls. Tears roll down her cheeks.

'I've got to go,' she tells Reshma quickly. She gets up.

'But—' Reshma says helplessly.

She runs out of Reshma's house.

Reshma calls behind her but Ladoo ignores her friend.

In blind rage and humiliation, Ladoo takes a rickshaw home, still clutching the diapers. She wipes her tears and ignores Reshma's calls. All she wonders is whether what Kavya just said is true. Is it too late for her to have a child? Is it too late for her to find true love? Is she going to remain a childless divorcee forever?

5

Ladoo reaches her colony, Swarg Lok, and tells the rickshaw driver to stop at the gate. She wants to walk home, so she has time to compose herself.

Clutching the diaper packet, Ladoo stops to wipe her tears and take a few deep breaths. She cannot let her family see her like this. She nears her house, still lost in thought, and opens the house gate. Billi, her dog, comes running out, passes her, and starts playing with another dog.

Irritated by this distraction, Ladoo yells out, 'Billi, at least don't flirt when you're pregnant, yaar!'

She hears a man's voice behind her, 'Why not? Maybe this dog is the father?'

Ladoo turns around in shock. It's Sandeep.

'Hi! Sandy? Hi!' Ladoo says, out of breath.

'Long time no see, Ladoo,' Sandeep says.

Ladoo smiles at him and nods. She has no idea how to talk to someone so handsome. There's an awkward second of silence.

'So . . . you're pregnant?' Sandeep asks her.

'Errr . . . no,' says Ladoo. She looks at her tummy, wishing she was thin like Sandeep's wife, and then realizes that Sandeep is looking at the diaper packet in her hands. 'Oh! Sorry! I thought you said I *looked* pregnant!'

Sandeep stares at her quizzically. 'No, you look great! As always.'

Ladoo blushes and says, 'Me? No! No!'

She shuffles awkwardly on her feet. Sandeep's eyes are the colour of the ghats after rain: brown, and soulful. She can't look into them without being drawn in. To fill the silence, she quickly holds up the diaper packet and adds, 'I won this as a prize at a baby shower.'

'Ah! Great. I love kids,' says Sandeep.

Ladoo is about to say so does she, when Sandeep adds, 'But my wife, Ira, doesn't want kids. She says they spoil a woman's figure and a man's bank balance. What's the point? So . . . no kids for us . . . I guess.'

'Oh, sorry!' Ladoo says slowly. She doesn't understand couples who can have kids but choose not to. To her, it's like saying no to a winning lottery.

'No biggie,' Sandeep continues. 'We have a dog . . . Rambo. We think of him as our baby. And, by the looks of it, he's having his own baby, so I'm going to be a dada.'

Ladoo laughs. Loudly. Sandeep looks at her in surprise.

'Hey!' he asks her. 'Are you okay? You look upset.'

Ladoo sighs and says, 'One of those days. I'll go home and drink chai. I'll be ok.'

'Adrak chai?' Sandeep asks, excited.

Ladoo smiles and says, 'Only adrak chai.'

'Adrak chai!' Sandeep repeats wistfully. 'Man, I miss chai. Ira's trying to lose weight. So we're only allowed to have black coffee at home.' Sandeep leans over and whispers, 'Can I tell you a secret?'

Ladoo nods. She can smell his cologne. It's intoxicating.

'Add a pinch of cinnamon to your adrak chai. Just a pinch. It's the best chai you'll ever taste, I promise!' he says.

'Really? Cool! Thanks for the tip!' Ladoo says.

She turns to go.

'*Chalo*. Bye, Sandy. Keep it tight!'

'Huh?'

'I mean, good night! Say hi to Ira.'

'I will! She'll be thrilled to know that she's becoming a *dadi*!'

Here's a man who loves his wife, Ladoo realizes, not a man looking to divorce her, as her mother claims. Sandeep's face flashes across Ladoo's mind and she crosses it out.

6

The next day, during lunch hour, Ladoo once again stands outside Bharosa Fertility Clinic.

As she stares at it, 410 comes up next to her and says, 'I can't take this any more, Ladoo. If not now, then never. Let's go inside and at least get a consultation.'

'No way!' says Ladoo.

'Do you remember what Kamini Kavya told you yesterday? Do you remember how much you cried to me about it on the phone? You have to do this.'

'I don't know, 410. Freezing my eggs? Or, worse, using a stranger's sperm? Having a baby this way. I never thought my life would come to this.'

'None of us thought our lives would be where they are now. And that's not necessarily a bad thing.'

'Everyone's life is perfect but mine. What have I done wrong?' asks Ladoo.

'You've done nothing wrong!' says 410. 'Look, I'll never say this again, but you're amazing! Ok? So stop feeling sorry for yourself. In fact, I feel sorry for myself. Why have you never asked me for my sperm? You think that Suresh's or

Ricky's sperm is better than mine? This is insulting. What have *I* done wrong?'

Ladoo laughs and says, '410, if I have kids with you, they'll come out looking like Appu Raja. They'll all be four feet ten inches.'

'Appu Raja? The dwarf dude in that movie? First of all, *so* politically incorrect. Second, that's really not fair! I'm five feet tall, not four ten. And I'm going to this acupuncture doctor on Badrinath Road. He's told me that I've already grown five centimetres, and I'll grow two more inches in the next six months! You watch! I'll be taller than you one day.'

'And, from that day, I will call you Sabu,' says Ladoo and bursts into laughter. She loves taking 410's case.

'Sabu is fifty feet tall! It's impossible to be that tall!' 410 says. 'So don't spoil Chacha Choudhary for me, you evil woman, and stop deflecting. We're going in.'

410 takes Ladoo hands and pulls her.

'No!' says Ladoo, resisting. 'I'm going back to office.'

But 410 opens the clinic door with his back and pushes Ladoo in.

'Come on. I can't take your indecision any more. You can never make up your mind about anything! We are doing this,' he says.

Ladoo straightens her back and glares at 410.

'We're doing this right now,' he tells her emphatically.

He walks over to the young receptionist sitting behind a desk.

'Hi!' 410 says. He peers at her name tag. 'Meera? An appointment for my dear friend, please.'

He points to Ladoo.

'For what purpose?' Meera says, not looking up from the file she's writing in.

410 looks at Ladoo. She has frozen in fear.

'Egg freezing, please,' 410 says. He giggles and adds, 'I never thought I'd use this term in my life! EGG. FREEZING. THANDA. ANDA.'

Meera's voice remains stoic as she says, 'Sir, egg freezing is known as mature oocyte cryopreservation. And this is not some silly biology class in school where you can giggle like a teenager. This is a place of business, and we are all adults here.'

410 stops giggling. Meera adjusts her sari *pallu*, without looking up, and adds in a monotone, 'Waiting period is three months. You'll have to come back.'

Ladoo turns to leave, but 410 holds her back firmly.

'My friend is desperate. Please!' he says.

'At Bharosa Clinic we do not use the word desperate, we use the word hopeful,' Meera says.

'In that case, I'm *hopeful* that you can do something for us,' 410 says, slipping Meera a Rs 500 note. 'Please?'

Meera looks up at them finally. Without blinking, she pockets the note and says, 'I've just received a cancellation. The doctor will be able to see you now, but you'll have to pay an emergency appointment fee of Rs 3000.'

'3000?' Ladoo shouts.

410 glares at her and says, 'What are you saving your money for? Ricky the dicky?'

'Ok, fine,' Ladoo says with gritted teeth. 'I guess I won't be able to buy that gold *bulaq* I wanted for my birthday now,' she mumbles under her breath.

'Bulaq is a traditional Pahadi nose ring,' 410 tells her, 'which means it's only meant for normal married women. So—'

Ladoo glares at 410. Then she pays the receptionist. Meera hands her a form. Ladoo fills it out. Meera takes the form from her and points to the waiting room.

'Nurse Asha will be with you shortly,' says Meera. 'Please wait there till then.'

410 and Ladoo sit down in the waiting room, in silence. After a few minutes, a nurse comes out and tells Ladoo to follow her inside to the examination room. Without 410. Ladoo looks woefully at 410, as she walks in. Nurse Asha tells Ladoo to step on the weighing scale. Ladoo carefully removes her shoes and gingerly steps on the scale. It shows 69 kg.

Ladoo looks apologetically at Nurse Asha and says, 'Actually I had chole bhatura for lunch. I didn't know that my weight would be checked today, otherwise I would've eaten cucumber or idli or something.'

The nurse doesn't react. She tells Ladoo to remove her salwar.

'I'm telling you the truth!' Ladoo continues. 'My weight is less than 67 kg. I swear! The salwar weighs at least 500 grams. My hair is also very long. It must weigh at least 500 grams. Hair has weight, right?'

Nurse Asha rolls her eyes and tells Ladoo to lie down on the examination table. She puts a white sheet over Ladoo's knees and stands next to her.

Ladoo looks up at the ceiling. She shakes her legs, feeling very nervous. Then, she sees a poster of a fat baby on the wall. It is smiling genially at her. Ladoo remembers why she's here. She smiles at the baby in the poster and stops shaking her legs. She has to do this!

The door to the examination room opens and she hears the nurse say, 'Dr Ma'am, the patient's name is Amara Joshi. She is here for MOC consult.'

Ladoo can't see the doctor's face, only her eyes. She says, 'Dr Ma'am, you can call me Ladoo. My dadi used to call me *lado* affectionately . . . but my sister Tammy would mispronounce it as *ladoo*. . . that's why it became my pet name. It has nothing to do with my weight, I promise.'

The doctor doesn't respond.

Ladoo continues to ramble, 'I'll tell you all my details. My age is . . . '

'Thirty-four,' says the doctor curtly.

'How . . . how do you know?' asks Ladoo, amazed.

Nurse Asha bends over and whispers into Ladoo's ears, 'Dr Ma'am can tell everything about a woman . . . just by looking at her vagina.'

'What?' says Ladoo in shock. 'How's that even possible?'

'Single?' asks the doctor.

Ladoo looks at the nurse, absolutely amazed. The nurse mouths, 'I told you. It's the magic of Sheilaaaa *ki jawani*.' She looks pointedly at Ladoo's vaginal area.

'Wow,' Ladoo mouths and turns towards the doctor in amazement.

She nods and says, 'Yes.'

'New to sex?' asks the doctor just then.

'Errr . . . I guess, Dr Ma'am,' says Ladoo shakily. 'I was saving myself for marriage, but my ex-husband was a little . . . er . . . a little bit impotent.'

'A *little* impotent?' asks the doctor sarcastically.

Ladoo says meekly, 'Yes. I didn't really have anyone else to compare him with. After my divorce, I met Ricky. He was my first. But he broke up with me, and—seeing that I'm here—he might be my last.'

Ladoo sees the doctor shake her head disapprovingly and mumble something about sex education in school.

'Then this will hurt,' the doctor adds, loudly.

Ladoo feels something wet and slimy go into her vagina. She pulls in her breath sharply.

'Sorry,' says the doctor. 'Just a few more seconds.'

To change the subject, Ladoo says, 'Dr Ma'am, I was wondering what the procedure is at your clinic? Whether we can freeze my eggs today itself?'

'I'm afraid we cannot freeze your eggs, today or later, Ms Joshi,' the doctor says curtly. 'Women who want to freeze their eggs come in when they're younger, twenty-six or twenty-seven years old. After that it's pretty pointless.'

Ladoo feels herself go stiff, as the doctor continues, 'I will not lie to you. The success rate of egg freezing is very low for a woman of your age.'

'Why?' asks Ladoo.

'In simple terms, the eggs will die during the thawing process. So why bother freezing them? Why make your body go through something pointless?' says the doctor. 'Don't waste your money. Or your time.'

'What? But, Dr Ma'am, this is my only chance to have a baby!'

'No, it's not,' says the doctor. 'You can always use donor eggs. From a younger woman. Or adopt.'

'No,' says Ladoo. 'I want my own eggs, my own biological child.'

'Then, what about surrogacy? Your eggs and donor sperm.'

'I want to carry my own child, Dr Ma'am,' says Ladoo softly. 'I know it sounds highly emotional and maybe selfish, but I want to experience pregnancy.'

'Please don't ever apologize for wanting a child, Ms Joshi,' says the doctor. 'It's your body, your life and, therefore, your rules.'

Ladoo nods in agreement and smiles. Dr Ma'am is amazing!

The doctor pauses and adds, 'In your case, taking into consideration all the factors and emotions, the only solution, if you're serious about having a baby, is to do artificial insemination.'

'Artificial insemination? IUI?' asks Ladoo, frightened. 'But that will require a sperm donor, Dr Ma'am. I don't want to do that.'

'It's totally your choice, Ms Joshi,' says the doctor. 'But, in my opinion, that's the best thing for you.'

Ladoo holds her head in her hands. She takes a deep breath and lets the doctor's words sink in.

'How much time do I have?' asks Ladoo slowly. 'If I do this?'

'I'll have to first take a look at your blood report to check your AMH levels.'

'AMH?'

'It measures your ovarian reserve . . . '

Ladoo looks confused.

'Your egg count. It is a fertility barometer,' says the doctor. 'But judging by what I've seen today, your AMH would be around 2.19 to 2.5. That's low to low–medium fertility. It's best if you get pregnant now.'

'Now?' Ladoo screams.

'Now,' says the doctor softly.

Ladoo shuts her eyes in disbelief. No, this cannot be.

The doctor pulls something out of Ladoo's vagina. Ladoo takes in a deep breath, but she is too shocked to feel any real pain.

'Now, for the good news. You're clear for STDs,' says the doctor. 'No cervical blockage. No PCOD. We can get you pregnant in your next ovulation cycle, which will be on . . . '

'12 July,' Ladoo says in a monotone.

'14 July,' says the doctor flatly. 'Your menstruation cycle has moved, your periods will be delayed by two days.'

'How do you know?' Ladoo asks incredulously.

The nurse again mouths, 'Sheilaaaa ki jawani.'

'Dr Ma'am, I am confused,' says Ladoo. 'If you're saying that egg freezing is not an option, then instead of artificial insemination, should I just wait till I meet someone?'

'Two of your eggs are dying as we speak, Ms Joshi, so . . . chop, chop. You had thirty-four years to do this the traditional way. Your fertility will drop drastically in the next few months. Frankly, you don't even have thirty-four weeks to spare.'

The doctor gets up and removes her mask.

'Nurse Asha will draw up your blood report. Meera will show you the sperm donor file,' says the doctor. 'She will take you through the process. We'll meet on 14 July for the impregnation. If you get pregnant, we will know by 2 August.'

'14 July? That's too early. I need more time.'

'Your choice. For now, we will start you on progesterone tablets because you'll have a geriatric pregnancy.'

'G . . . g . . . geriatric? As in the kind meant for old people? But doctor, I'm only thirty-four!'

'A thirty-four-year-old childless woman in India is geriatric. We don't have American eggs that become geriatric after forty.'

Ladoo doesn't know what to say. She just stares at the doctor in surprise.

'We will also prescribe you folic acids,' adds the doctor.

'Doctor . . . I'm already taking those . . . to prepare my body,' says Ladoo earnestly. 'That's how much I want to get pregnant.'

She sees the doctor look at the nurse and then walk out.

Nurse Asha glares at Ladoo and says, 'If you've been preparing your body for pregnancy, then why are you hesitating now? Make up your mind, man!'

Ladoo looks at the floor, not sure what to say.

The nurse continues, 'Are you in or out? Remember, Ladoo, your biological clock is ticking—tick-tick-tick-tick-tick-tick!'

Nurse Asha leaves. Ladoo puts on her salwar and walks out of the room. She finds 410 waiting for her eagerly, next to Meera's desk.

'So?' he asks enthusiastically. 'Has your anda become thanda?'

He grins at Meera, who rolls her eyes.

Ladoo shuffles on her feet and says, 'Apparently it's too late for me to freeze my eggs. My Sheila ki jawani has become a *budhi rani*. I should've taken better care of my health.'

'Come on, stop being so critical of yourself, Ms Joshi,' says Meera.

'I have to take the next step,' Ladoo continues, in a daze. 'I have to . . . get pregnant now.'

'What? Now?' 410 asks.

'Now,' says Ladoo.

'Jai Bholenath!' says 410, sympathetically. 'You must be freaking out!'

Ladoo nods. She is.

'Hey! Cheer up!' says 410. 'You were doing all this to have a child anyway! Why wait? Might as well get right to it! No?'

'But what about finding love, 410? What guy will marry me if I have a child through a sperm donor?'

410 makes Ladoo sit down.

'Look, Ladoo, think rationally. I know men,' he says. 'If they love a girl, they will not care if she has a child, or whose child it is. The man you choose should love you for who you are, without any conditions.'

'You think?' asks Ladoo.

'Yes!' says Meera.

They both look at Meera. She turns away, embarrassed at being caught eavesdropping, and begins getting a file ready for them.

'You've dated losers, so you don't know good men,' 410 continues. 'They treat women right, with respect and maturity. There are not a lot of us, but there are enough. Trust me, don't let finding true love hold you back from getting what you truly want: a child.'

'You're right, 410,' Ladoo says. She takes a deep breath.

'You can do it,' 410 says.

'I know, 410,' says Ladoo. 'I know I *have* to do it. I *want* to do it. But I don't know if I'll be *able* to do it.'

'Ok, chill! This is obviously a lot to process, for anyone! Give yourself some time. Let it sink in. Till then let's understand what we're getting into. Maybe get a second opinion?'

'Why?' Meera butts in again. 'Dr Ma'am knows what she's talking about. People from all over the world come to her.'

'Meera is right,' says Ladoo. 'Dr Ma'am makes Rs 3000 in five minutes. That's Rs 18,000 in one hour! No one but a genius gets paid that much.'

'Clearly, you're not one,' says 410, 'because that's Rs 36,000 per hour, babe. Your maths is as weak as your andas.'

Ladoo ignores his jibe and says, 'I don't make that much in one week.'

'Thank God your job has nothing to do with numbers,' 410 says sarcastically.

This time, Ladoo punches him in the arm. 410 yelps in pain.

A few patients in the waiting room turn to look at them. Meera glares at them. They quieten down.

Meera places some brochures in front of them and says, 'Here are our packages for IUI. Bronze package: Indian sperm. Silver package: NRI sperm. Gold package: Foreign sperm.'

'Is there a diamond package for alien sperm?' 410 asks.

Meera does not smile. Ladoo kicks him under the table.

'I would recommend the gold package for you, Ms Joshi,' Meera continues. 'We have fresh foreign sperm from the tourists who come to Rishikesh!'

Ladoo studies the brochures for some time, hears the nurse's tick-tick-tick-tick-tick-tick, then turns to 410 and asks, 'Do you think I should do it? Use a sperm donor? Become a single mother?'

'Sushmita Sen is a single mother and she's awesome. As is Neena Gupta. You'll never be as hot as them, obvs, but you can be cool like them,' says 410.

Meera says, 'Ms Joshi, all the women in this clinic come with their husbands or partners. You've come with . . . *this*.' She glares at 410. 'You'll be our clinic's first single mother. So, we have a special limited time offer for you. If you pay Rs 50,000 more for a gold package . . . you can get premium gora sperm: blue eyes, blonde hair, exactly like Hrithik Roshan. Imagine how gorgeous your baby will be! Beautiful baby means less lonely mummy. No?'

Ladoo and 410 look at each other in shock and laugh.

7

'Hrithik Roshan? I would love for my baby to look like him. But he's desi, not gora!' Ladoo tells Tamara that evening, as she lights a diya for the Ganga aarti at Triveni Ghat.

'Indians think all *chikna* people are goras,' says Tamara.

'So, what should I do?' Ladoo asks her. 'Should I do it?'

'Do it, Dids! You've wanted this since three years.'

'I don't know, Tammy. What if I can't get pregnant? What if I'm not a good mother? What if I can't handle being a single mother? What if something happens to me, and the child becomes an orphan? What if I meet someone while I'm pregnant? What if—'

'Stop it, Dids. You were ready to have a whoopsie pregnancy and marry that idiot Ricky. You think *he* would have made a good father? You think you would have been happy with him? You're better off being a single mother than being married to a man who is not right for you.'

Ladoo looks out at the ghat. Tamara is right.

'It's not fair, Tammy. All I wanted was marriage and kids, like any normal girl. And look at how tough both things have been for me. Why am I so unlucky? Why do I have to go out of my way to get what other girls get so easily?'

'Dids, doing things differently means you're original, not a copycat. So, stop whining. Be proud of your journey!'

'You're totally right, babe,' says Ladoo, with a smile. 'But . . . I don't know. It's a bit too unconventional.'

'Dids, you're divorced, Bua is unmarried, and I'm a nonsense-value social media star. We're already an unconventional family. Trust me, no one will be surprised.'

Ladoo sighs, 'Oh God! I forgot about that! What will people say?'

'Who cares what people say? Are they paying our bills?'

'I guess I'll be able to deal with people. But what about Maa? Papa? Bua?' Ladoo asks her sister softly. 'Especially Maa? She is not going to like this one bit.'

'What have I always told you, Dids? Be the kind of girl who does not take tension but gives tension. I'm there. I'll handle them. Even Maa.'

'I wish I was as bindaas as you, Tammy,' says Ladoo sincerely.

'There's only one thing stopping you from being bindaas, Dids. And that's you.'

They finish the aarti and walk up the ghat steps. Ladoo still looks unconvinced. 'Maybe Dr Ma'am is wrong. I read a news report that a sixty-five-year-old woman gave birth to a child.'

'Your bodies are different. There are women in their twenties who can't conceive, and women in their forties who can easily conceive.'

Ladoo nods at her younger sister's wisdom.

'Still, I don't know. I'm not that old, na? I don't even feel old. I feel like I'm still sixteen,' says Ladoo. 'I'm sure I can wait.'

Suddenly five–six kids come running towards Ladoo, shouting, 'Didi! Didi!'

'Ugh!' Tamara says, eyeing the kids with disgust. 'Every time these neem pakoras show up.'

Tamara tries to swat them away like they're flies and shouts, 'Go away!'

Ladoo ignores her sister. She feigns surprise and then laughs as she fishes lollipops out of her purse. She hands them over to the kids. This is her daily ritual. The kids shout, 'Love you, Didi,' and run back to play.

Tamara's face softens as she sees this.

'Don't be confused, Dids. You belong with children,' she says. 'And I'm fed up. I'm waiting to be a *masi*. Maybe that way I'll like at least one kid.'

Just then a girl bumps into Ladoo. She turns around and says, 'Sorry, Aunty!'

Ladoo's jaw drops. 'Aunty? Aunty?? When did I become an aunty? I'm thirty-four, not fifty-four!'

She turns to Tamara, 'Oh God, Tammy, do you think I have wrinkles? Do you think my Sheila ki jawani has wrinkles? That's why Dr Ma'am told me to not wait? Oh my God, I *am* an aunty and no one even told me!'

Tamara looks at Ladoo like she's batshit crazy.

'What's wrong with you, Dids? Chill. You're not an aunty!'

But Ladoo looks frantic. Tamara drags her sister into Café India, as Ladoo continues to rant: 'You know what . . . 410 is older than me . . . he's thirty-eight . . . but he's not scared about his—' she circles her crotch area '—Shahenshah, even though, after forty, Shahenshah is not a baap, but a baap re baap. No one talks about the male biological clock, only the female one. Tick-tick-tick-tick-tick-tick! The world is so unfair.'

Everyone in the café stares at Ladoo.

Tamara grabs her sister by the shoulder and says softly but firmly, 'Dids, you can change the world later, focus on yourself now.' Tamara points to a sadhu outside. He is doing Trikonasana. 'Do what he's doing. It will help you calm down.'

'I don't need to be calm. I need to be fertile. Will doing asanas help me become the world's most fertile woman?' Ladoo asks.

Just then an American walks up to Tamara and asks if she's the 'Hot Yogini' from Instagram. And if he can buy her coffee.

'Sure, one frappuccino with whipped cream for me, and one kahwa chai, no sugar, for my sister! She's on a diet right now,' says Tamara. She poses for a selfie with the American—she's done this a thousand times before—while keeping an eye on Ladoo, who is now looking longingly at a baby who is being burped on her mother's shoulders.

'Errr . . . is she allowed to diet in this state?' the American asks Tamara seriously. He's looking at Ladoo's stomach.

Tamara facepalms and whispers, 'My sister is *not* pregnant.'

Too late. Ladoo has heard him.

'I have water retention, okay?' Ladoo snaps at the guy and walks out of the café in a huff.

Tamara runs after her, 'Dids, you are really losing it. That guy didn't mean any harm!'

'Of course I'm losing it, Tammy!' says Ladoo in frustration. 'In the last few hours, I've been told that my fertility is low, that I'm an aunty, and that I look pregnant.'

Tamara looks at her sister and grins, 'I think it's a sign from the universe that you might as well get pregnant.'

Ladoo looks irritated for a moment and then realizes the irony of the moment. She grins back slowly. Tamara stops and holds her sister by the shoulder. 'Dids, I think it's time.'

Ladoo looks at her helplessly. She takes a deep breath in. She looks at the beautiful ghat in front of her. 'You're right. You're right. I have to do this.'

Tamara nods.

'But, Tammy, I'm scared. Making Shahenshah meet Sheila is going to be tough. Probably the toughest thing I'll ever do in my life.'

'Dids, you've lived in Rishikesh all your life, but never gone white-water rafting or bungee jumping, because that's what *really* scares you. That will be the toughest thing you do, not this! Not something you've wanted all your life.'

'One day, na, I'll go to Recovery Point and do that bungee jump! You'll see,' Ladoo says and smiles. 'But, jokes aside, if I do this, I'm going to need you, Tammy. Will you be there for me? Through everything?'

'Always, Dids,' Tamara nods and hugs her sister. 'Sisters are there for each other through all seven lives, so what's one? I promise to be your life partner in sin.'

Ladoo smiles. 'I'll have to speak to Maa, Bua and Papa as well. I'll need their support as much as yours.'

'Of course! Should we go home now and tell them?' asks Tamara.

'No. Give me a few days to process this,' says Ladoo. 'Let me gather the courage.'

'Good idea. Till then let's get on their good side! Because, frankly Dids, only Bholenath can help us now!'

8

The next few days, Ladoo and Tamara do everything to make a good impression on their parents and Bua. They wake up early to go to the Shiv–Parvati temple with their mother. They buy her favourite Hajmola bottles. They make tulsi chai for their father and accompany him on his evening walks. They buy him a Kindle so he can listen to audiobooks. They buy non-stick pans for Bua, who loves cooking, but always ends up burning the food. They fast without complaining every Monday. Tamara cleans her room without her mother having to tell her. Ladoo meets the boy her mother has set her up with. They let their mother and Bua watch Big Boss every night without interrupting them.

When Ladoo goes to AIIMS hospital to see Reshma's newborn baby, she realizes it's time for her to have her own. She comes back home, looks at Tamara, and says, 'I'm ready. Let's do this.'

*

The following Sunday, the entire Joshi family gathers on the terrace. It's *jadoo ki jhappi* day, where they all take a break from their morning routine, so that Mrs Joshi can massage their hair with coconut oil.

Tamara is sitting on a stool, holding a doll. Her mother is on the mirchi gadda massaging Tamara's hair. Bua is hanging up clothes, her favourite activity. Mr Joshi is playing an audiobook, *his* favourite activity, that they're all listening to, while waiting for their respective turns. Ladoo enters the terrace, carrying bowls of gajar ka halwa for everyone and kahwa tea for herself.

'I'm making your mother listen to *Beti Ka Dhan*, Premchand's epic story,' Mr Joshi tells Ladoo. 'It's a beautiful story about a father who is abandoned by his sons during a crisis, but then saved by his daughter who sells her jewellery.'

'Daughters are the best,' says Tamara with a grin.

'Your papa knows how much I love books, even though I can't read. This is his way of showing love,' adds Mrs Joshi. She looks at her husband affectionately.

Tamara indicates to Ladoo to broach the subject with her parents. Ladoo opens her mouth, but nothing comes out. She puts down the tray on the gadda and turns to go. As she's about to walk out, Mrs Joshi yells, 'Ladoo beta, give me a bite of the halwa. My hands are oily. And looking at Tamara's hair, getting longer and longer, I will be sitting here forever.' She grumbles but her voice is filled with fondness.

Ladoo puts a spoonful into her mother's mouth.

'Yes, Dids. Sit,' says Tamara. 'It's your turn next.'

Ladoo sits on a chair next to them. She takes a sip of the kahwa, avoiding the halwa she loves, but dutifully feeding it to her mother.

Tamara glares at her and says, 'Why don't you tell us how you've been, Dids? What's *new* in your life?'

Ladoo glares at Tamara, but no one is paying them any attention. She looks around to make sure that Kamini Kavya is not there. Finally, as Mrs Joshi is about to finish, she says softly, 'Maa. Papa. Remember . . . the other day . . . at the dining table . . .'

'Arré, speak fast, Ladoo,' says her mother impatiently. 'I have to make breakfast also. This Tammy has eaten all the halwa.'

'Err . . . remember, how I spoke to you about egg freezing and artificial insemination the other day?' Ladoo adds, a little more firmly now.

'What?' asks her father. He pauses the audiobook. 'What assimilation?'

Ladoo opens and shuts her mouth like a fish, but no words come out. She can't do this!

'Artificial insemination, Pops,' Tamara chimes in, running out of patience. 'Basically, everyone, Dids wants to have a baby that looks like Hrithik Roshan.'

'Hrithik Roshan?' her mother says, 'Isn't he with Suzanne?'

'No, Mom, he's single,' says Tamara. 'And he's now going to have kids with Dids and . . .'

'Stop joking about this stuff, Tammy,' Ladoo interrupts her. 'Maa. Papa. Bua. I need to say something . . . that . . . a . . . I—'

'Get to the point, beta,' says her mother. She's not understood the gravity of what Ladoo is saying.

'I tried to talk to you last night,' says Ladoo. 'But you said I was making you miss Rashami's love song with Asim.'

Mrs Joshi looks at Bua, 'Obviously, na? You cannot disturb Bua and me when we're watching Big Boss.'

'Ok, sorry. What I wanted to talk about was . . . ' Ladoo takes a deep breath and blurts out, 'I'm having a baby now . . . without getting married . . .'

'What?' says Mrs Joshi.

The bottle of oil she is holding falls to the ground. It splatters all over Tamara. Ladoo watches as the dupatta Bua is hanging slips out of her hand, and her father spits out his tea.

'That came out wrong! I'm not pregnant,' Ladoo adds quickly. 'But I am planning to have a baby using a sperm donor.' She feels awful but she knows she has to say it. 'Basically, I met a fertility doctor in order to freeze my eggs. But she said that my fertility is low, so—if I want a child—I need to have one immediately. Since marriage is not on the cards, presently, I'll have to have a child without getting married.'

'Beta, what nonsense are you talking?' says her mother. 'A woman has to marry to have a child.'

'No, Mom. Women don't need husbands to have children,' says Tamara.

'Tammy, you keep quiet,' Mrs Joshi snaps at Tamara. 'I tolerate your nonsense because you say it's part of your job on social media. But this is real life. We cannot take it lightly.'

'Maa,' Ladoo butts in. 'I . . . I know this is shocking . . . but Dr Ma'am told me I cannot afford to waste any more time.'

'Then why are you wasting our time with this nonsense? Do you even know what you're saying?' says her mother. 'First you got divorced. We didn't say anything, even though we were not happy about the nuisance value of it. We even *allowed* you to move back and live with us.'

'Allowed me? Maa, this is my house! And I am not a nuisance!'

But Mrs Joshi is not listening. 'Now you want to have a child without marriage? This is too much. Do you know what people will say about you? How they will treat your child? This is not America or Mumbai, Ladoo. This is the land of spirituality, of God. There is respect for morals here; traditions need to be followed and values need to be observed. You cannot go around doing characterless things.'

'Characterless?' says Ladoo angrily. 'I'm not murdering someone, or raping them, or robbing them! I'm having a baby! How is that characterless?'

To diffuse the tension, Tamara pulls Mrs Joshi's hand towards her head to force her to keep massaging her hair. But Mrs Joshi is too upset. She swats Tamara's hand away.

Ladoo looks up from the ground and says, 'Maa, try to understand. There is nothing I want more in this life than a baby. I don't have an alternative, Maa. Trust me, I've tried. But I'm getting old.'

'Old? My friend Rita is pregnant at fifty! She makes you look young!'

'Maa! My body is not her body! It's not your age, but your health that matters when it comes to having a baby. My biological clock is ticking, faster than Rita Aunty's. I have a very small window left to have my own child.'

'And whose fault is that? I made you meet such nice boys but you kept rejecting them,' says her mother.

'I've told you, Maa, that I can't do another arranged—'

Tamara holds Ladoo's hands to calm her down and speaks up, 'Mom–Pops, last time you kinda forced Didi into an arranged marriage. See what happened. Didi has suffered so much already. She's been in trauma for five years. Now she wants to do something nice. She wants to fulfil her dream of becoming a mother. She needs you. Please support her?'

'Don't blame us for Ladoo's divorce. How were we to know her husband was a good-for-nothing druggie?' says Mrs Joshi.

'Beta, it's not like we're forcing Ladoo to get remarried,' Mr Joshi says, looking like he's finally recovered from the shocking news. 'It's her choice.'

'But that doesn't mean that she can go and do whatever she feels like,' says her mother.

'Ok, Mom,' Tamara says. She again pulls Mrs Joshi hands to make her continue massaging her head, hoping it will calm her. But Mrs Joshi gets up and looks at her younger daughter. 'And think about yourself, Tammy. You also have to get married. You are almost thirty! Who will marry you if your sister is an unwed mother?'

'Don't worry about me, Mom. I've told you that I'm never getting married! I have better things to do,' says Tamara.

'Really?' asks her mother. 'What's better for a woman than getting married?'

'Everything! Since we're all being honest here. I'm thinking of moving to Mumbai, to become a big social media influencer. I will not have time to have kids. Anyway, having kids is so . . . so middle-class,' says Tamara.

'Don't talk nonsense, Tammy,' says her father.

'Hey! All I'm saying is that this is your *only* chance to have a grandchild,' says Tamara. She smiles at everyone, as if she's won the argument for all of them. They all glare at her. She stops smiling and looks sheepishly at the ground.

'This is all *your* fault,' Mrs Joshi tells Bua. 'You have spoilt these two girls with all your Western ideas. Letting them watch *Friends* and *Game of Thrones* and what not.'

'Bhabhi, I was watching those shows to learn English!' Bua says. She looks as shocked as the rest of them. Then, to avoid Mrs Joshi's deathly stare, Bua quickly bends down to pick up the dupatta she had earlier dropped.

'Think about it, everyone,' Tamara continues. 'Dids has never done anything wrong. She's listened to you, even when it made her unhappy. She's never made a big decision in her life without considering you first. Making this family happy is her priority. You know that.'

They all look at each other. It's true.

'Plus, she'll need you,' says Tamara. "Cause I don't know how to look after babies.'

Tamara purposely drops the doll she's holding. The doll's head detaches and rolls to Mrs Joshi's feet. They all look at it in shock.

'Stop your nonsense, Tammy. Do you want your sister to ruin her life? To do this awful thing and go from being called Ladoo to Badnam Ladoo?' asks her mother.

'Bhabhi, people talk. Even if you're good and you're nice to them, they still talk. Why do we care?' says Bua. 'If Ladoo thinks this is a good idea then maybe it *is* a good idea.'

'Mina . . . ' Mrs Joshi says warningly.

'I agree with Bua,' says Tamara. 'Mom, if your only issue is with what people will say, then we can pretend that Dids adopted, or did surrogacy. During her pregnancy we'll move out and rent a flat in Mumbai. There are many girls like Dids there, at every coffee shop, at every gym, even the lesbian . . . I mean Lebanese ones. Or we can move to Shimla for one year, you know like Kareena Kapoor in *Jab We Met*. Let's not complicate something that is simple.'

'This is not one of your movies, Tammy. Don't talk rubbish!' says Mrs Joshi.

'When you can't get ghee out with a straight finger, you have to use a crooked finger. Didn't you teach us this, Pops?' asks Tammy.

'I did,' says Mr Joshi, nodding his head. '*Waise*, it's not a bad idea, Padma. I think it can be done. We'll not tell anyone what's going on. Ladoo will go away, so that no one finds out. This way we'll avoid a scandal, and Ladoo will get what she wants. You and she will both be happy. And we'll get a grandchild. Everyone wins!'

'Have you lost your mind, ji?' Mrs Joshi tells her husband.

'Maa, don't you trust me?' says Ladoo. 'Have I ever done anything to make you feel ashamed?' Her mother doesn't reply. Ladoo turns to her father and says, 'Papa, thanks for supporting me. I promise you that no one will find out that I'm pregnant. But I will not move to Mumbai or Shimla or anywhere. I'll stay here. I cannot be away from home, from all of you.'

Mr Joshi nods his head and says, 'Fine, Ladoo. You figure out the correct way. But no one must find out. That's my *only* condition to support you. Is that fine?'

Ladoo nods.

'Promise?' he adds.

'Promise,' Ladoo says.

Mrs Joshi looks at all of them like they're crazy. 'What is wrong with all of you? Are you all really this foolish? This naïve? You want to bring a calamity to our house?' She turns to Ladoo and Tamara. 'I refuse to be a part of this Westernized and uncultured nonsense. I really wish I had a daughter like Kavya instead of you two!'

'Maa, please,' Ladoo says desperately. 'I kept an open mind when you set me up with all those boys. I did it for you. Can't you also be open-minded? For me?'

'A woman shouldn't open her mind so much that her brains fall out, Ladoo,' says her mother in anger.

'Maa, you supported Billi when she had her four puppies a few days ago? So, why not me?' asks Ladoo.

'I had to give away two of Billi's puppies to my friends, because we can't afford to keep them,' says Mrs Joshi. 'That is the life of single mothers—whether they are dogs or humans. Sacrifice! And more sacrifice. Is that what you want?' Without waiting for a reply, Mrs Joshi picks up the bottle of oil and stands up. 'I suggest you start fasting every Thursday.'

'What? Why? I already fast on Mondays because you tell me to,' Ladoo says.

'Fasting two days will knock some sense into you. It will help you get married faster. You are clearly losing your mind without a husband!'

Saying that Mrs Joshi leaves the terrace.

'Ouch!' says Tamara.

'Don't get upset, Ladoo. I'll speak to Maa. This is too much for her,' says Mr Joshi, getting up from his chair. 'But beta, are you 100 per cent sure about all this?'

'Pops, having a child is like having to do potty,' Tamara tells her father. 'You got to do it when you got to do it.'

Mr Joshi makes a face at Tamara's choice of words.

'What she means, Papa,' Ladoo says earnestly, 'is that I know what I'm doing is *hatke*. But you keep telling us that India will progress when its women progress. So, shouldn't a woman decide when and how she wants to have a baby? Does motherhood have to mean marriage? Or can a woman only have a child within the confines of marriage?'

'Beta, you are a woman I am proud to be the father of. But we both know the rules are different for women. Let's not sugar-coat this. People will judge you a lot more. They'll make your life difficult. You have to be absolutely certain you want to do this. Because there's no going back from this. Children do not come with a refund ticket. Nor does a bad reputation.'

'Don't you keep saying that I'm like the son you never had, Papa?' says Ladoo. 'If your *son* wanted a child, without marriage, would you have stopped him?'

'Children are never stopped by their parents, Ladoo, or we wouldn't raise them, we'd fail them,' says Mr Joshi. He walks up to Ladoo and looks at her with a small smile. 'You're old enough to know what you're doing.'

Ladoo hugs her father in delight. 'I love you, Papa.'

'Yes, yes,' Mr Joshi says, shuffling on his feet, unaccustomed to such displays of affection. 'Don't smile so much. I've agreed only if no one finds out.'

When he leaves, Ladoo collapses on the mirchi gadda. She can feel her heartbeat quickening and beads of sweat forming on her forehead.

Tamara comes up to her, 'You did it, Dids! You told them!'

Ladoo turns to her sister. 'Jai Bholenath! That was the most difficult conversation I've ever had. But you were amazing, Tammy! Dropping that doll! Genius!'

'I told you I'll take care of you. I know more shit than Google does.'

'But where did you get that doll from?' Bua asks Tamara.

'It's Kavya's daughter's doll, I assume,' says Tamara.

'Or son's. Let's not be sexist,' says Ladoo.

'Or son's,' adds Tamara. 'I saw Kavya cleaning up her kids' toys from the terrace this morning. She's not the only one who's allowed to spy. She left this doll, so I jumped across to their terrace and borrowed it.'

'You mean *stole* it?' says Ladoo, looking at her sister with concern.

'Shabash, beta,' Bua tells Tamara.

Ladoo looks up at Bua and asks, 'Bua, don't you think I'm the one who deserves a shabash?'

Bua comes and sits next to Ladoo. She looks into Ladoo's eyes with a smile and says, 'Do you know that thirty years back when I found no one to marry, I wanted to adopt a child? But Bhabhi refused. Same reason: What will people say? Till today the biggest regret of my life is not that I didn't get married, but that I listened to Bhabhi and didn't adopt a child.' She pauses. 'I'm with you. You deserve this.'

Ladoo hugs her. 'Really? Thanks, Bua.'

'But before you choose any boy for this . . . irrigation . . .' says Bua.

'Insemination.'

'Insemination thing . . . I'm going to get his *kundali* made to see if it matches yours,' says Bua. 'That's my condition. If thirty-two or more *gunas* match, only then you have my blessings!'

'What?' Ladoo says, laughing. 'Matching kundalis with sperm donors! Bua, seriously?'

'Arré! I'm your bua and I'm also hatke!' Bua says proudly. 'It's the matter of a baby, my grandchild. We must follow some traditions, at least!'

Ladoo laughs and says, 'Ok . . . we will match horoscopes and only then go ahead!'

'Bua, thanks for saying yes. We need you,' says Tamara.

'What about Maa?' says Ladoo.

'Don't worry about her,' says Bua. 'We'll convince her. If she doesn't relent, we'll tell her after you get pregnant. She'll have no choice then.'

'Don't worry, Dids. Focus on the one ally you need now: a kundali-matching sperm donor!' Tamara says.

Bua looks at Ladoo seriously and adds, 'We . . . we're doing this, right?'

Ladoo takes a deep breath. 'Bua, like you said. I'll regret not doing this more than I'll regret doing it. So, yes, we're doing it! I'm going to make you a *badi nani* and Tammy a masi.'

'Yay!' says Tamara.

Tamara and Ladoo hug each other.

Tamara pulls away and picks up the doll. 'Now let's give this stolen . . . I mean borrowed . . . doll back to its original owner: Kamini Kavya.'

She throws the doll to the adjacent terrace and makes a run for it.

[illegible] and I [illegible] match [illegible] then we have my blessings!'

'What, Father say anything, Madam [illegible] [illegible]

'And [illegible] your husband [illegible] said. 'But [illegible] proudly [illegible] the [illegible] [illegible]. We must allow [illegible]

[illegible] and only [illegible]

'Tara, thanks for saving us. We need to leave, Tara.'

'What about [illegible]

[illegible]

[illegible] she [illegible]

[illegible]

[illegible]

[illegible]

[illegible] Tara.

'Tanu and I [illegible] each other.'

[illegible]

[illegible]

9

A few days later, Ladoo is at Bharosa Fertility Clinic with Tamara and 410.

Meera pulls out a thin file and says, 'This is your donor file, Ms Joshi.'

'Please call me Ladoo,' says Ladoo. She looks at the file sceptically and asks, 'Meera, are you sure this is the complete information of all the 100 donors?'

'Of course,' says Meera. 'As per company policy, we cannot reveal more about the donor's identity than this. Remember, donors are anonymous.'

Tamara turns the pages and adds, 'But this only has the donor's date of birth, qualification, caste and childhood photo. How will Dids decide whom to choose based on such little info?'

'It's not little. It's more than enough,' says Meera. 'Trust me. Use your imagination. Look at the donor's childhood photo and you'll get an idea of how your child will look.'

'I don't know,' says Ladoo.

'Remember, we're Indians. We are quite imaginative,' adds Meera. 'If you throw us out of a train, like they did with Gandhiji, we'll throw you out of the country.'

They all look at Gandhiji's photo hung up on the wall.

'You like Gandhiji?' 410 asks Meera flirtatiously.

Meera replies equally flirtatiously, 'I like Gujaratis!'

410 raises his eyebrows and says, 'Really? *Hum Gujarati chum*!'

Meera says, '*Hum janum chum!* I know.'

Ladoo kicks 410 under the table, to stop him from flirting, and asks, 'Can't you make an exception, Meera, and give me the donor's name or job or address or personality or family history . . . any relevant information?' She is still not convinced.

'Their names are as good as Gautam Patel's,' says Meera, 'and their addresses are such that you better avoid Dehradun, Israel and all Eastern European countries, if you don't want your child falling in love with their brother or sister, because that's where most of these donors are from!'

'You know my *real* name, Meera?' asks 410 slowly.

'Yes, Gautam Patel,' Meera nods and smiles at 410.

'But didn't you hate me the last time we met?' he asks.

'I did. Then I realized that you're doing such a sweet thing for your friend. You must be a nice guy. And I like to know everything about nice guys!' says Meera.

They smile at each other. Ladoo rolls her eyes. She flips through the donors' résumés and begins to read some of them.

Meera interjects, 'Actually, Ms Joshi . . . I mean Ladoo. People usually take this file home and then read it.'

'If she takes this home, she'll not come out alive,' says 410. 'Her IUI is a big secret.'

Meera nods. She understands.

'In that case, let me help you. It'll be very quick.'

Meera holds up a few sheets at a time, 'These are Marwaris. Punjabis. South Indians.'

'Too stingy. Too loud. Too nerdy,' says Ladoo. 'If possible, please show me only the Kumaoni donors. Otherwise, my mother will be even more upset!'

'Ok,' says Meera. She removes some papers. 'Now you're down to just eighteen candidates. That was quick, right?'

'Yes, thank you,' says Ladoo gratefully.

'What's the next criteria to help you decide?' asks Meera.

'Oh! I know!' says Tamara. 'Bua had told me to call her when we had shortlisted the candidates. She's waiting outside in the market only.'

Tamara dials Bua's number and updates her. Within a few minutes, Bua walks into the clinic with a pundit. Everyone turns to stare at them. The patients. The nurses. Even Ladoo's Dr Ma'am.

Meera tells 410, 'In all the time I've worked in this clinic, I've never seen a sight like this. It's like shaadi-type feels.'

Bua sits down beside them and asks the pundit, 'Punditji, will you be able to match the kundalis using only the date of birth, caste and qualification of the men?'

'Of course,' says the pundit. 'Anyway, it's not like anyone selects a groom on the basis of his looks!'

'That's true! Let's begin by chanting Bholenath's name,' says Bua.

'Jai Bholenath,' they all say.

The pundit looks at the horoscopes for some time and then says, 'These ten boys match the thirty-two gunas.'

'Jai Bholenath!' says Bua. 'My Ladoo has found a match!'

She distributes mithai to the stunned crowd.

The pundit leans over and asks Meera, 'By the way, what kind of clinic is this?'

10

That night Ladoo has a terrible dream. She dreams that her baby is born, a son, and she's very happy. She names the child Barfi. But when he grows up, Barfi asks her who his father is. Because she doesn't know, the baby turns into a weed-smoking, bansuri-playing unemployed idiot, like her ex-husband Suresh. Ladoo wakes up in a sweat, with the haunting sound of a kid chanting: *Suresh Papa Suresh Papa Suresh Papa*. She decides, there and then, that no matter what, she will meet her sperm donor, so she can tell her baby who his/her father is.

*

The next day, during lunch, 410 is standing outside the clinic, staring at it. Ladoo pushes him in.

'If not now, then never,' she says.

410 rolls his eyes and says, 'How the tables have turned.'

Meera smiles when she sees 410 walk in.

'Hi!' she says.

'Hi! You're looking very pretty today,' 410 tells her. 'Have you lost weight?'

Meera giggles and says, 'And, you're looking very tall today. Have you gained height?'

'I have,' says 410, looking mockingly at Ladoo. 'Thanks for noticing.'

Ladoo ignores their flirting and gets to the point.

'Meera, please help me. I have to know the father of my child.'

'What?' says Meera.

'Please!' says Ladoo.

'You know I can't, Ms Joshi,' says Meera.

'Ladoo, please call me Ladoo.'

'Well, Ladoo. That is classified information. I will lose my job.'

Ladoo nudges 410, who is gazing cutely at Meera.

'Please, babe,' says 410. 'Do something!'

Meera clears her throat.

'Of course,' says 410. He whispers, 'Is twenty enough?'

Ladoo whispers fiercely in protest, 'Are you mad? I'm not rich like you!'

'You're rich also, 410?' Meera says tantalizingly. 'You're really the complete package, aren't you?'

Ladoo sighs and says, 'Will Rs 5000 do? Please!'

'Rs 15,000,' Meera says stubbornly.

'Give some discount, na, please?' says 410.

Meera smiles at him and says, 'Ok. Rs 10,000. Final. Only for you.'

Ladoo rolls her eyes. She transfers the money via Paytm to Meera's account.

Meera prints out a document.

'Promise me that you'll never reveal how you got the names,' says Meera. 'Not only will I lose my job, but the doctor will lose her practice, and the clinic will shut down. You can't let other women miss out on their dreams to fulfil yours. Ok? Promise?'

Ladoo promises her that the donors will never find out. Meera hands her the printout.

'But listen, Meera. I cannot do the IUI till I meet my donors and decide whose baby I want. So, can we postpone my IUI? Can we do it two months later, so I have enough time to meet them?'

'Sure,' says Meera. 'But, Ladoo, we have a strict vetting process for donors. You really don't need to meet them.'

'Trust me, I do. I have terrible luck with men. I don't want my child to have the same. I want my child to have a good father, even if he or she doesn't know who it is.'

*

Ladoo is on her laptop at office with the donor sheet in front of her. Her first screening process involves stalking her potential sperm donors online. She rejects Harish Bohra because he supports Donald Trump on Twitter. She rejects Mohan Joshi because he has an incomplete LinkedIn profile, showing that he's not worked since college. She rejects Bipin Bisht because Google shows him as a harasser in the #MeToo movement. All this takes her exactly twenty minutes.

'Strict vetting process, my ass,' mumbles Ladoo to herself.

She crosses out all their faces in her mind, one by one.

410 suddenly appears in front of her. She is startled.

'What mischief are you up to?' he asks her suspiciously.

She makes a face at him.

'Never mind,' he says. 'You're missing the buzz in office.'

'What buzz?'

'They want a co-anchor for my show, as it's become quite popular. Brokers in Mumbai are going crazy over it.'

'That show *Rishi Kesh to Rishi Cash*? Good for you! Now you'll get marriage proposals from Mumbai as well. Congrats!'

'Congrats to you too! Because I've recommended your name as my co-anchor.'

'What? No way!'

'Why is everyone saying that?'

'Is this a joke?'

'No.'

'I can't do it, 410. I can't be an anchor.'

'What? Why not?'

'Because I'm not anchor material, 410. I'm not skinny or pretty.'

'Hey,' he says angrily. 'Why do you keep whining like Nirupa Roy all the time? You are beautiful. And smart. Smarter than anyone else in this office, if I don't count your maths skills.'

'Dude,' says Ladoo, 'why do you always do things for me out of pity?'

'Pity? Mad or what, Ladoo? The only thing I pity you for is your pathetic taste in men!'

'Do you have a point?'

'Yes, you're doing this,' says 410. 'And you're going to kick ass.'

Ladoo leans over and whispers. 'Listen. I know your papa owns this company and everyone will do whatever you say, but you are aware that I'm going to get pregnant and fatter and uglier and weirder?'

'Wow, you haven't heard a word I've said!' says 410. 'You are going to rock this job. And, you know what, I'll bump up your salary by 10 per cent if you do it. You can use that money to pay for baby expenses. And, there will be a lot, if it's your baby!'

'410! Thanks, but no thanks. I've already lost my fertile eggs because of this job. I can't put in more time . . . '

'We're doing this. Remember, you always say that "a journalist is a journalist . . ."'

' . . . only on camera.'

'Exactly. Dry run in forty minutes. See you in the studio!'

Ladoo rolls her eyes and says, 'Studio? When did we get a studio?'

Forty minutes later, on the way to the black curtain and makeshift desk that 410 calls 'studio', Ladoo grumbles, 'No one but him can imagine me on TV.' She doesn't need his handouts, she decides. But she can't say no to him. She remembers the first time she'd met 410 in school, twenty-three years ago. She was eleven years old and he was four years her senior, as well as the school head boy. He had caught hold of a bully, Hemant Chauhan from Shimla, who was teasing Ladoo in the canteen about her weight. 410 had made Hemant apologize to Ladoo in front of everyone and made him promise that he would never tease someone because of their physical attributes. Due to his height, 410 knew bullying. But he had not only survived it, he had thrived in it. He was the most popular boy in school, and—since that incident—Ladoo's idol, though she never let him know that. They'd been best friends ever since, and their friendship had survived bullies, crushes, jobs, marriage, and everything else life had thrown their way.

So—Ladoo records the show with 410, hoping he'll realize that she's a disaster. But she's not. She enjoys anchoring, and 410 and she have a natural chemistry.

Ladoo joins 410 as the co-anchor of *Rishi Kesh to Rishi Cash*, and loves every minute of it.

*

However, the show is the least of Ladoo's priorities. She has something bigger planned for herself and this involves 'accidentally' bumping into the rest of her seven potential donors, outside their offices and homes. She knows where these men work, where they live, how they commute, and who their friends are. She's going to spy on them without them finding out!

After all, the best way to know someone is to watch them when they don't know they're being watched. She ignores Tamara's 'stalker' taunts and decides to dedicate her weekends to this task.

So it begins. She rejects one donor because she sees him digging his nose in a tanga. She sees the other one push an old woman while trying to get into a bus. The third one is married, and she realizes his kids are obnoxious brats. He's out.

She crosses out all of their photos in her mind, one by one.

Ladoo is down to only four donors now. She decides to line up 'dates' with the other four men to get to know them properly.

*

To meet the first guy, Manish Singh, a yoga teacher, Ladoo creates a Tinder account, as his Facebook status says he's on the app. She goes through many profiles, till her fingers almost fall off from swiping, before she finds Manish. She swipes right. Within a second they are matched. Hooray!

Manish asks her to come with him to watch a movie, *Murder 4*. He seems smart and funny, till the intermission, when—as they're eating popcorn—he tells her that he loves movies about murderers because he comes from a family where his *chachu* stabbed his dada, and his *phuphi* added poison to his *taya*'s tea. He adds that since they're Jats these things keep happening. Ladoo hands Manish the bag of popcorn and leaves. She deletes Tinder from her phone and crosses out Manish's photo in her mind.

*

Ladoo tries to remain positive. After all, her kundali still matches with three more potential donors. There is still hope. She spies on the second guy, Kunal, a travel agent, on his LinkedIn profile. He seems to be an avid dancer, so Ladoo joins a bhangra class at the Bollywood Dance Academy that he's a part of. This time, she takes Tamara for support. They both stare at Kunal doing bhangra.

'Cute, na?' Ladoo asks Tamara. 'Could he be Mr Right?'

'Mr Right *Donor*, Dids,' says Tamara. 'But his kid will come out doing bhangra! Look how overenthu he is.'

Ladoo sighs dreamily, 'He is, isn't he?'

'Before making him the father of your child, go talk to him,' says Tamara.

Tamara waves to Kunal. She catches his eye and points to Ladoo. Kunal leads Ladoo to the dance floor. He tells her to follow his dance moves. Ladoo picks up a little bhangra. She has a great time with Kunal. *Could he be the one?*

She's going to find out soon, because he asks her out for dinner.

They go to a small restaurant. Kunal is looking at the menu and Ladoo is looking at him, adoringly.

Kunal mumbles something.

'What?' Ladoo asks him.

'Papa, will you have lassi?' he says.

Ladoo shifts uncomfortably on her chair. 'Err . . . my name is Ladoo, not Papa.'

But Kunal is looking at the seat next to Ladoo's.

'How can you order the paneer makhana? You know your BP is high,' he continues.

'Whom are you talking to, Kunal?' she asks him, looking around.

Kunal looks at her with sad, sincere eyes, 'Can't you see, babe? It's my father.'

This sends a shiver down her spine. Kunal had told her that his father died four years ago.

'Isn't he . . . you know . . . ' she says.

'Maybe for the world, but not for me. Papa never left my side, not even in death, because he loves me so much,' says Kunal. He stops and nods, as if he's listening to someone. 'Papa is saying he likes you, Ladoo. You want to say hi to him?'

'Namaste, Uncle!' says Ladoo quickly, to the air.

She adds that she needs to go to the bathroom and runs out of the restaurant. She shudders as she crosses out Kunal's photo in her mind.

*

Tamara and Ladoo are sitting at a table in Café India. Ladoo is primping and putting on lipstick. Tamara looks at her sister in shock.

'This is it,' Ladoo says. 'We are down to our last two donors. Varun Joshi, a research fellow at AIIMS hospital, and Bunty Sahu, a junior engineer at a factory. And one of them is going to be my child's father.'

'I know, Dids. But let me get this straight. You send a friend request to both these donors, and then called them both *together* for a date here?'

Ladoo looks at her sister evenly.

'Yes and no,' Ladoo says. 'I called them both . . . here . . . but two hours apart. I need to get a little stricter about my vetting process. You know, after Kunal . . .'

' . . . and Manish and Ricky and Suresh . . .' says Tamara cheekily.

Ladoo glares at her. 'I'm not like you . . . always single and . . .'

' . . . loving it,' says Tamara.

'The plan is to ask them both the same questions, intelligent and revealing questions, and see who does better. That's why I need to meet them like this,' says Ladoo.

'What kinds of questions are you going to ask them?'

'Family history, personal habits, food they eat, their views on religion, how they treat women, and whether they believe in ghosts. I want to stop being a psycho magnet and become a smarto magnet.'

'Intense,' says Tamara. 'But, who knows? Maybe your Mr Right Donor also turns out to be Mr Right?'

'Maybe,' says Ladoo. 'Now leave. Varun has come. Observe him, and later Bunty, and tell me slay or nay, ok?'

Tamara quickly gets up and sits at the next table. She watches her sister on her two dates.

'Your family: COVID positive or negative?' Ladoo asks them.

'We told Corona . . . ' says Bunty.

' . . . don't bore us, na?' says Varun.

'Mental health: Kangana or Alia?' asks Ladoo.

'Alia, of course,' says Varun.

'But Kangana is hot!' says Bunty.

'Women: *abla nari* or *krantikaari*?' asks Ladoo.

'Krantikaari,' says Bunty.

'But behind every krantikaari was once an abla nari,' says Varun.

'Murder movies or romance?' asks Ladoo.

'Romance,' says Bunty.

'But every murder begins with romance,' says Varun.

At the end of each date, Ladoo looks at Tamara. She says slay for Varun and nay for Bunty. Ladoo nods in agreement. She likes Bunty, he is nice, but he doesn't make her laugh the way Varun does. He is not intelligent or insightful like Varun. She wants Varun's qualities in her child. She crosses out Bunty's photo in her mind, and smiles at Varun, the father of her soon-to-be child.

*

A few days later, when she's ovulating, Ladoo goes to the clinic with Tamara, Bua and 410. Holding the Gita in her hand and chanting the Gayatri Mantra, she gets inseminated with Varun's sperm.

She has to wait three weeks to know if she's pregnant. To take her mind off this, Ladoo tries to continue her life as normal. She plays chess with her father on the terrace. She goes with her mother to meet two boys, in the hope that Mrs Joshi will get appeased, because she hasn't told her mother that she's doing IUI. She prays every morning at the Shiv–Parvati temple, asking for a child. Tamara pats her stomach all the time, as Bua feeds her gondh ladoo. 410 fills her cup with haldi doodh when they co-anchor.

Ladoo also goes on dates with Varun. They take ferry rides to Geeta Ashram and laugh over badam kulfi. Ladoo likes him.

Three weeks pass. Ladoo goes to the terrace bathroom to take a pregnancy test. Tamara, Bua and 410 wait outside, tense. Ladoo comes out crying. The test is negative. The insemination didn't work! Ladoo is not pregnant.

Dr Ma'am confirms this. Ladoo is shattered.

In grief, Ladoo stops taking the folic acid pills. She stops reading pregnancy books. She stops highlighting baby names in her favourite books. She refuses to eat Bua's gondh ladoos or drink 410's haldi doodh.

Meera convinces her to try again, the month after next. Ladoo reluctantly repeats the IUI process. This time she doesn't go anywhere for those critical three weeks, not even to office. She stays at home, forcing herself into bed rest, because she thinks this will increase her chances of pregnancy. She tells her mother she's on leave and spends her time listening to books on her father's Kindle.

This time Ladoo does not do a home test, but goes directly to the clinic. She waits nervously as Nurse Asha tries to find a beating heart, a little seed, in the sonography. There's nothing. The silence is deafening. The test results are negative again. Ladoo is not pregnant!

Ladoo lies on the examination table, without moving, asking herself: will I ever get pregnant?

The clinic wall behind her gets darker and darker, till it's black.

*

Three months pass.

One day, 410 calls up Tamara.

Tamara is doing a live video on Insta on how to straighten one's hair at home. She answers, annoyed, '410, not a good time.'

'Tammy, have you seen Ladoo?' 410 asks in panic. 'She left office early to get her test results and didn't come back.'

Tamara cuts her live and puts down the hair straightening product she's holding.

'What? She told me she'll wait till evening to go, so I could go with her!'

'I also told her I'll go with her, since this was her third IUI. But she sneaked out when I was in a meeting. I went to the clinic later to find her, but she was gone.'

'Shit! We know what that means!'

'Look, her phone is switched off. Maybe she's at home?'

'Wait,' says Tamara. She runs from room to room. 'Let me find her.' After a minute, she adds. 'She's not at home.'

'If she's not at home, office or the clinic, where is she?' asks 410.

After a short pause, they both say together, 'Shit!'

*

There are signs saying 'Bungee Jumping' everywhere. At Recovery Point, the tourists are long gone. The place is empty. 410 and Tamara trek up the hill. They are panting.

Finally, they spot Ladoo. She's sitting alone with empty beer bottles around her. There are dark circles around her eyes that are puffy from crying. Ladoo sees them and laughs.

'I did it, guys!' she shouts, as if they're sitting in her living room. 'I jumped! But I didn't feel anything. No fear, no thrill.'

'That might be because you're drunk,' says Tamara, clutching her stomach that is cramping from the uphill walk. She picks up the bottles and says, 'Dids, you are so careful about your diet. Why are you doing all this now?'

'Because there's no point, is there? My body has let me down,' Ladoo snaps. 'Look at yourself. You eat so much and you eat everything . . . samosa, halwa, pizza, chocolate. You don't even exercise. Yet, you are thin. I'm so careful . . . yet I'm fat . . . and . . . and infertile. Why bother any more?'

'Stop this body shaming, yaar,' says 410. 'It's not ok, it's not healthy.'

'Seriously, Dids,' says Tamara. She removes her shawl and wraps it around Ladoo.

'But it's ok, guys,' slurs Ladoo. 'Because it's *my* body. I can say whatever I want about it. Because the truth is that whenever I hold my test results in my hands . . . I hate myself . . . and my uterus . . . for letting me down. My marriage failed. My career failed. And, now, my body has failed. I'm a loser. I'm not worthy of being loved or even loving someone. That's why God is punishing me.'

'Dids, stop it!' says Tamara. 'Stop being hard on yourself. You cannot give up so quickly.'

'Quickly? I did everything I could. I took so many injections. Injections! Can you imagine! I had so many progesterone tablets and fertility drugs. I prayed every single day at the temple. And what did I get for all of this? Negative. Beta. HCG.'

'Dr Ma'am told you it can take time. That you have alternatives,' says 410.

'What alternatives? She told me today that the only option I have is IVF. That means more injections, more medicines and more hormones!' Ladoo pauses and takes a big gulp of beer. 'And more money. Do you know how much one round of IVF costs? Rs 3 lakh! Can you imagine . . . 3 lakh! I've already spent Rs 4.5 lakh on this . . . shit!

I've broken all my FDs, mutual funds, to raise the money. I have nothing left.'

Ladoo pauses. She takes another sip of beer.

'Everyone is leading normal lives and I'm trying to conceive,' she tells Tamara. 'Maybe it's a sign from God that I should give up. I'm too old. By the time I'm fifty, my child will be like . . . twenty-five years old.'

'Fifteen . . . ' says 410 gently.

'Fifteen?' says Ladoo. 'That's even worse! I might die and my own child will be left an orphan. Why would I do that to a child? Why?'

'You're still young, Dids. *Cosmo* says that thirties are the new twenties,' says Tamara, trying to cheer her up.

Ladoo laughs, 'Actually, thirties are the new forties and forties are the new fifties. Because our eggs can't go to the gym to work out or get facelifts and Botox. They get old before us. Thanks to our stress levels, they dry up before we do. That's why many women get menopause in their early forties!'

'Stop it, Ladoo. You're an ordinary person doing something extraordinary,' says 410. 'It's great! Give yourself some credit, and kindness.'

'No, man. Kamini Kavya was right. My train has left the station,' says Ladoo. 'Even in *Badhaai Ho* they make fun of that poor old mother. Maa was right. This is not natural. So, stop your lies and go away!'

Ladoo pushes 410. He falls but immediately gets up.

In Amitabh Bachchan's voice, 410 says, '*Mard ko dard nahin hota*!'

'Mard?' says Ladoo. She pinches his nipple; he squeals. 'You are a man, aren't you? You go! No men are allowed near me today.'

'Eh? What did we do now?' asks 410.

'Like a tsunami, hate is rising in me for your whole manly gender. You didn't give me the cow—fine! But now you're not letting me have the milk also? Kaminon! You men are the cause of all my problems. So, I will not let your kind grow. I will never tip any rickshaw-wallah or scootsy-wallah or male waiter . . . ever.'

'I'm . . . I'm sure we men will be devastated by this *great* loss,' says 410. 'Drink some water now.'

Ladoo falls to the ground. Tamara picks her up.

'Dids, don't blame mard. Or your body! Find a solution. Do the IVF,' says Tamara. 'Many women have done it. You can too!'

'Do you have any idea how painful it is?' Ladoo asks.

'No!' says Tamara. 'But, what's the alternative?'

'There is no alternative. Dr Ma'am told me that our ovaries produce our eggs. And the eggs mine are making are not gooey golden motichoor ladoos, but sad sugar-free wheat ladoos. I have no other choice but IVF. But where will I get the money from? Papa is an honest income-tax officer—I don't know why—and has no money.'

'That's the problem? Money?' Tamara says. 'I have the money. I'll give it to you.'

'Or me,' says 410.

'You man, you go,' Ladoo tells 410. He shrugs his shoulders and refuses to move. Ladoo turns to Tamara. 'How do you have so much money?'

'I know you all think I do nothing. Just eat the whole day and take selfies on my phone. But I have a serious career as a social media influencer. For every brand endorsement, I get Rs 10,000 to Rs 30,000. I've saved all that money in my bank account. Dids, I've learnt this by reading your articles on personal finance and savings!'

'Really?' says Ladoo. 'I cannot believe this. You read my articles?'

'I'm half your readership base,' Tamara teases her.

'Can you spare this much?'

'Who do I have to save for?'

Ladoo laughs, 'You've turned out to be quite the *chhupi-rustam*. Why didn't you tell me you're rich?'

'Dids, the more people underestimate you, the easier it is to rise in their eyes. This is my life *ka funda*!'

'And it's better than Ladoo's anda,' says 410.

Ladoo whacks 410. They both laugh. Tamara wraps herself in Ladoo's shawl, as Ladoo leans on her shoulder.

'But what if I do the IVF and fail . . . again?' Ladoo asks them. 'This is my last chance! I will not be able to take another hit.'

'A last chance is called a last chance because it's the first breakthrough,' says 410. 'Give it a shot, Ladoo, and make your last chance your best chance.'

'If not now then never, right?' says Ladoo and smiles.

410 nods and smiles. He hugs her.

'There you go!' says Tamara. 'Tomorrow we will call up Dr Ma'am and tell her the Joshi sisters are ready for IVF!'

Yay, they all say together.

410 snuggles into the shawl with the two sisters. They all hug.

'Tell me something, Ladoo,' 410 asks. 'You didn't bungee jump, did you?'

'Not a chance, mard,' says Ladoo. They all laugh.

11

There are cries and protests behind the bathroom door. Ladoo is bent over the sink, cringing in pain. Bua is fanning her with her dupatta. Tamara is holding an injection next to Ladoo's lower back. She brings the needle close to her sister's skin. Tamara's hands shake.

'I can't! I can't! I can't!' says Tamara.

Ladoo shuts her eyes and says, 'You have to! Come on! Come on, Tammy!'

'Nurse Asha showed you how to do it, right? Do it exactly like that,' says Bua.

Tamara loses her nerve and says, 'How can I possibly do it? Dids is shaking. She looks like she'll faint.'

Ladoo snaps, 'Obviously I'll faint if you take so much time.'

Suddenly they hear Mr Joshi's voice, 'What's going on?' They jump in shock. Tamara drops the injection on the floor. He comes to the bathroom door. 'The whole colony can hear you! What are the three of you up to now?'

Tamara and Bua look down in shame. Ladoo picks up the injection.

'Papa, I have to take injections for my hormones, FSH and LH, for the IVF treatment,' says Ladoo. 'Every day, twice a day.'

'Since it was Ladoo's IVF today, Nurse Asha told us to take the injections at home for the next two-three weeks. These can double Ladoo's chances of getting pregnant,' says Bua.

'Nurse Asha even showed us how. I thought I could do it, but it's very tough,' says Tamara.

Mr Joshi looks at Ladoo with pity. He gives his Kindle to Bua to hold, washes his hands and rolls up his sleeves.

'Beta, you've been scared of needles since you were a little girl,' he says. He takes the injection from Ladoo's hand. 'Who gave you injections then?'

'You,' says Ladoo sheepishly.

'Now you've grown up and forgotten your Papa?'

'No, Papa. I thought you'd not be comfortable about all this.'

'But I've been supporting you, beta. I also want to be a *nanu*.'

He smiles at Ladoo.

'But Maa?' says Ladoo.

'Don't worry. She's still at Kavya's house.'

Ladoo thinks about this and adds, 'Ok. Please . . . gently!'

She lifts her kameez. She's sweating. Mr Joshi softly begins to sing *Lakdi Ki Kathi*. Ladoo smiles on hearing her favourite childhood song. She holds Tamara's hand as the needle goes into her back. A tear rolls down her cheek. Bua sniffles. She can't see Ladoo in pain.

'Chalo, it's done,' says Mr Joshi. 'I'll do this every day for the next three weeks. Ok? Are you okay?'

Ladoo nods. Mr Joshi wipes the tear from Ladoo's cheek. 'I'm happy to feel needed by you again,' he says. 'I miss that with you girls grown up.'

Suddenly, there's a sound by the door. They hear Mrs Joshi's voice, '*Sunoji*, Kavya has personally requested that I sit at the mandap during her brother's wedding *pheras*. What an honour! Her mother will die of envy!'

Mrs Joshi enters the bathroom. She sees them all and steps back.

'What's going on here?' she asks.

They all stare at her in shock. Mrs Joshi turns to Mr Joshi and asks, 'Deep?'

Mr Joshi takes a gulp. He's never lied to his wife before, and he can't start now. 'Nothing, Padma. Since . . . errr . . . Ladoo . . . is doing . . . IVF . . . we are . . . '

'What?' says Mrs Joshi. She turns to Ladoo. 'IVF?'

She pauses. 'I told you to not try these stupid things. But you did. You were lying to me all this time? Making a fool of me?'

'Maa, I'm sorry. I didn't want to upset you,' says Ladoo. She takes a deep breath. 'But don't worry about it. I'm not getting pregnant anyway. Something is wrong with my body.'

'Serves you right, beta,' says Mrs Joshi coldly.

'Padma!' says Mr Joshi.

'Why are you stopping me, ji?' Mrs Joshi tells her husband. 'Have I said something wrong? If Ladoo gets pregnant, will you treat it as good news or bad news? Will you tell people with pride, or will you hide it from them?'

Mr Joshi looks away uncomfortably.

'It's something so shameful,' Mrs Joshi continues, 'that I can't even tell Kavya about it. And you? You may treat your daughters like sons, but you've forgotten that if anyone finds out the truth, people will lose respect for you overnight. You'll not get that promotion you're expecting, to become a commissioner. Everything you have worked for your entire life will be wiped out. You know this, right?'

'Mom? Pops didn't know about the IVF,' Tamara jumps to her father's defence.

Mrs Joshi turns to her younger daughter, 'And you? I let you eat eggs at home in sin. I let your short clothes, your reputation, your stubbornness to not get married . . . all that slide, to support your ambition of being famous. So that you can go to Mumbai and become an influencer or whatever. I have done *everything* I thought would make you happy.' She stops to wipe a tear. 'And what have you done, Tammy? You've taken advantage of me being open-minded. Of my love? Of my trust? Aren't you ashamed of yourself?'

Tamara begins to cry. Bua holds her.

Mrs Joshi turns to Bua and says, 'And Mina? When Bapuji threw you out of the house and you came to stay with us, not once did I treat you like a sister-in-law. I always thought of you as my sister, more than even your own brother did. I never let you feel unwelcome. I gave you everything you asked for. I didn't let any guest stay over even for one night, so that your room could remain yours. I watched Big Boss with you. I drank with you, my life's only sin, so you didn't feel lonely. I did everything for your happiness. And, in return, you've spoiled my daughters. Do you know how to be a responsible adult, or are you always going to act like a silly, immature dependent?'

Bua starts crying. Ladoo looks like she's going to faint.

'The four of you don't know what you're doing,' says Mrs Joshi. 'You're destroying our sweet family, our sweet home!'

'Maa, I'm sorry,' says Ladoo, wiping a tear. 'This is all my fault. Not theirs.'

'I know that, Ladoo,' says Mrs Joshi. 'And, let me tell you. Kavya is not my daughter, but she respects me more than my own do. She listens to everything I tell her. She shows me unconditional love.' She pauses. 'Do whatever you want. I have nothing to do with it. From now on, I disown you as my daughter. Understood?'

'No, Maa,' Ladoo screams. 'Don't say that. Please!'

But Mrs Joshi turns around and walks out of the bathroom.

'Go to hell, all of you,' says Mrs Joshi in fury. 'You've seen my love, now you see my anger.'

Mrs Joshi leaves. Ladoo faints. They all run to hold her.

The empty IVF injection lies on the bathroom tile.

[illegible] and night, so that your mom [illegible] will [illegible] [illegible] with you. I don't know [illegible] only do so you'll [illegible] thing for your happiness. And [illegible] quitted my daughter's. Do you know how [illegible] [illegible] like [illegible]

[illegible] looks like [illegible] going to [illegible]

'[illegible] don't know what you're doing,' says Mrs [illegible] [illegible]

'[illegible]' [illegible] This is all [illegible]

'I know that, Lalita,' says Mrs [illegible] 'Let me tell you [illegible] but [illegible] [illegible] She [illegible] I [illegible] you as my daughter-in-law.'

Mr [illegible] 'Then [illegible]' [illegible] and walks out of the room.

'[illegible],' says [illegible] 'You've [illegible] before the [illegible]'

Mrs [illegible] Lalita [illegible] they hold hands.

The [illegible] bathroom [illegible]

12

Over the next few days, Ladoo waits at the door for her morning walk with Mrs Joshi, but her mother doesn't show up. Ladoo goes to the Shiv–Parvati temple alone. She buys shakarkandi for her father alone. Tamara stops eating eggs in fear of Mrs Joshi. She trades her usual shorts and ganji for a sari to impress Mrs Joshi, but her mother ignores her. Mr Joshi waits in their room to make Mrs Joshi listen to a new audiobook, but she ignores him. Bua puts on Big Boss every night and pours a peg for them, but turns it off as Mrs Joshi doesn't show up. Mrs Joshi—an excellent cook—stops cooking, so Bua takes over, and they have to eat her burnt food. The whole family waits on the terrace on Sunday for their head massage, but Mrs Joshi does not come. Everyone is sad as they miss their Mrs Joshi.

Three weeks pass. At midnight, one day, 410 enters Ladoo's house. Tamara is sitting alone by a birthday cake. Mr Joshi is drinking alone. Bua is holding a banner which reads: HAPPY 35th BIRTHDAY, LAADLI LADOO. They all look sad and lost.

'Is this a funeral or a birthday party?' asks 410, 'Where's the birthday girl?'

They point to Ladoo's room. 410 goes in. There is total darkness.

Tentatively 410 says, 'Happy birthday, laadli Ladoo! Where are you?'

Ladoo doesn't reply. 410 walks around blindly and then turns on the bedside lamp.

He sees Ladoo lying scrunched up in her bed, with a blanket till her nose.

'See your gift,' 410 says slowly. 'I got the gold bulaq that you wanted . . . remember?'

Ladoo doesn't look up, but replies in a monotone, 'I thought that was only for married women?'

410 laughs nervously, 'Are you any less than a married woman?'

Ladoo starts weeping. She turns off the lamp. 410 looks confused as Tamara enters the room.

'What did I say?' he asks Tamara. 'I'm sorry. Sorry, sorry!'

Tamara turns on the lamp and whispers, 'It's not you. Since morning Dids has been saying—'

'I'm thirty-five years old,' Ladoo cries. 'I don't have a husband. I don't have a child. My mother hates me. My family is fighting because of me. I'm such a loser!'

Ladoo pulls the blanket further over her head. Her phone buzzes. 410 and Tamara look at it.

'Dids, Varun is calling you again. He's your boyfriend. At least talk to him,' says Tamara.

'Let Mr Right Donor make the right donation first,' 410 whispers sarcastically.

'Shhh, 410!' says Tamara. 'Dids, tomorrow your IVF results will come out, and they'll definitely be positive. You'll become a mother and Varun a father. Don't make him suffer like this. Take his calls!'

'I don't care about the results any more. Can't you see how many problems have been caused because of my stupid donor nonsense? Honestly, I don't want any test results any more! I don't want Varun any more! I don't even want to get pregnant any more!'

Ladoo turns off the lamp.

410 whispers, 'Hormones! I think she's already pregnant!'

'Shut up ya, 410!' says Tamara. 'Dids, don't say all this! Think positive.'

'Yes! It's your birthday, yaar!' says 410. 'You'll only get good news.'

'I wish I hadn't started all this,' Ladoo whispers. 'I've hurt everyone I love. I'm going to die alone, and I deserve it!'

410 whispers, 'We don't need the results. Laadli Ladoo is definitely pregnant! Now we know that her anda was not thanda.'

'Don't talk too much,' says Tamara. 'Do you know that there's a male biological clock as well . . . tick-tick-tick-tick-tick-tick!'

410 stares at Tamara in alarm, as she grins mischievously at him.

*

The next morning 410 enters Ladoo's house again. Tamara is still sitting alone by the cake. Bua is still holding the banner and Mr Joshi is still drinking alone, only this time it's chai.

'Waah!' says 410 sarcastically, 'The Joshi family does not like change does it?' He smiles at them. No one smiles back. 'I've been trying Ladoo's number since morning. Have the results come?'

'No one knows! She's switched off her phone,' says Tamara.

'Ladoo hasn't left her room since yesterday,' says Bua.

'But don't blame us for being party poopers,' says Tamara. 'We are ready to celebrate if Dids is pregnant. See.'

She holds up a banner that says CONGRATS!

'And if she's not pregnant?' asks 410 slowly.

'Then I'll cut this banner and it'll become—'

Tamara holds up half the banner that reads RATS!

'Rats?!?' they all say together.

Tamara giggles. They all smile at each other.

410 says, 'Finally, some joy.' He pauses. 'Anyway, what are we waiting for? Let's find out the results.' He dials a number. 'Hello, Meera?' he says flirtatiously, '*Kem cho*?'

410 leaves the hall and comes back after a minute. They're all standing up, tensed. He walks up to Tamara. He holds up the full banner, so it reads CONGRATS! Ladoo is pregnant!

They all jump up in excitement! They hug each other! They hoot and cheer! Bua bows before Lord Shiva's photo. Mr Joshi wipes a tear. Tamara takes a photo of the confirmation report Meera has sent 410 on WhatsApp and is about to post it on Insta, when Mr Joshi stops her.

They walk into Ladoo's room holding up the banner. They hug Ladoo as 410 shows her the report. Ladoo stares at the report in disbelief for a minute, till the truth sinks in. She then jumps up in happiness and hugs them all! They make her sit down. Ladoo cries and laughs at the same time.

'I don't believe this! I don't believe this!' she says over and over again, and strokes her tummy gently. Tammy kisses it.

Ladoo says a prayer, 'Bholenath, thanks for giving me the best birthday gift an almost middle-aged woman can ask for!'

Ladoo finally comes out of her room. She bows before Lord Shiva's photo and then cuts her birthday cake. She goes around with a slice of cake and everyone takes a bite each. She then cuts an extra slice and puts it on a plate. Everyone looks at her in surprise.

'It will not feel like good news till I tell Maa,' says Ladoo.

The others look at each other sceptically.

'Beta, is that a good idea?' asks Mr Joshi.

'Papa, you'll see!' says Ladoo. 'Maa will forget her anger once she hears my good news.'

'Hopefully she will not call it the terrible, horrible, very bad good news,' says 410 and chuckles.

Everyone looks at him and then turn to look at Ladoo. They know that's exactly what Mrs Joshi will call it.

Still, Ladoo leaves them, and goes up to the terrace. Mrs Joshi is playing with Billi's two puppies.

Ladoo watches her for a moment, and then smiles and says, 'Maa? Congrats! You'll be a nani soon!'

Mrs Joshi doesn't react. Ladoo sits next to her and gives her the plate.

Mrs Joshi puts the plate down on the floor and gives the cake to the puppies.

'Maa, please,' Ladoo says in desperation. 'For the sake of your grandchild, please forgive me.'

'Forgive you?' her mother says, very slowly.

She is silent for a minute. Ladoo stares at her mother. What's going on in her mind?

Then, Mrs Joshi asks, 'Do you know why I named you Ladoo?'

'I thought it was because Dadi—'

'No. I told you that because I was ashamed to tell you the truth,' says Mrs Joshi. She takes a deep breath. 'As you know, I grew up in Nainital. My parents didn't have much money. My father was a schoolteacher. We were eight children. Eight! Many times there wasn't enough food in the house. So, my father would beg our local *halwai* for his leftover cooking oil. My mother would tell us that the oil tasted of motichoor ladoos. We kids would drink it and say that one day we would eat real motichoor ladoos. Since then, I have associated ladoos with success and respect. That's why I called my first child Ladoo. To never forget how far I've come.'

Mrs Joshi wipes a tear. Ladoo's eyes fill up. Mrs Joshi has never told her this.

Mrs Joshi adds, 'I am uneducated, because my father had no money to send me to school. Not even the school he was teaching in. Imagine the irony! That's why I gave you girls all the opportunities I didn't get—from a good education, to working and building a career, to choosing when and whom to marry—to escape the label that an uneducated mother cannot raise successful children.'

Her mother's voice breaks. 'And I know I've put a lot of pressure on Tammy and you to succeed.' She's shaking with emotion. Ladoo tries to hold her mother, but Mrs Joshi pulls away.

'But now,' Mrs Joshi adds, 'you're trying to destroy all the respect I've built through my hard work. You were the first person in our family to get a divorce. And now you want to do another shameful thing. What face will I show to people? I look at Kavya and wonder why you cannot be like her.'

'Maa, please don't say that.'

'Why not?' retorts her mother. 'Is it too much to ask? I've always abided by rules and had a good life. Rules are good. Rules are there for a reason. Because they've worked for centuries! Rules help us avoid pain. So, who are you to break all the rules that society has set? Why are you messing with something that has been established as wisdom?'

'Maa—' says Ladoo gently.

'Especially when you know how women are judged? When you know that being a woman means following society's rules!'

Ladoo doesn't know what to say.

'I am saving you, Ladoo. From making a big mistake. Please stop this nonsense. It's not too late,' her mother continues. 'You can get an abortion.'

'Maa! How can you even say that?' Ladoo says angrily. 'You can love your dog's babies but not your daughter's?'

'When people found out that I was having another girl, they told me to abort her, and try for a boy, so my family could be "complete". I didn't. Instead, I decided to raise my daughters as I would have raised my sons. With dignity and ambition. As equals. I invested all my hopes in my two daughters. I thought everything I could do, my daughters would do better! To me my family was complete. But you . . . you have spoiled everything.'

'I haven't, Maa.'

'Do you think Bua, Tammy, Papa and that 410 will always be there for you, Ladoo? That they'll help you raise your child? Have any of them given birth? Do they know how much hard work it takes to raise a child? They'll go back to their lives after the novelty wears off. You'll be left alone. Remember that.'

'Maa, forget all this. Please,' says Ladoo placatingly. 'Today is a good day. Except that you forgot to wish me for the first time ever?'

'A mother can forget every date but not her child's birthday. After all, that's the day she's born as a mother.'

Mrs Joshi gets up and says, 'I will never forget that day. I remember every detail. How I was alone when you were born. How your Papa was posted in Lucknow at the time. The labour pain, delivery, nursing, stitches, the sleeplessness. I did it all alone. It took a toll. I used to wish I'd die . . . or that you would.'

'Maa!'

'You guys call it postpartum depression today, right? We didn't know such fancy terms. Raising a child is the toughest thing a woman does, Ladoo. How will you do it alone? It is not possible. It is not worth it.'

'I'll manage, Maa,' says Ladoo, taking her mother's hand in hers.

'I will disown you if you do,' says Mrs Joshi, letting go of her daughter's hand.

Ladoo starts to cry. How will she ever convince her mother?

'Maa, please forgive me,' she whimpers. 'Please be there for me.'

But Mrs Joshi walks out of the terrace. Ladoo falls to the ground.

She doesn't see Kavya standing behind the clothesline. Kavya has heard everything! She is smiling, a thin, long, evil smile.

Kavya picks up her phone and dials a number.

13

There's a kitty party in progress at Kavya's house. There are housewives in saris chatting away. Mrs Joshi enters. She looks happy. But her expression turns to one of surprise when she sees the other women look at her and whisper. Some snigger. Mrs Joshi waves to her friends, Gunjan, Helma and Savita, but they turn away.

Uncertain, Mrs Joshi places two bowls of chole on the dining table. She sees an identical bowl of chole next to it. She picks the bowl up in surprise and asks, 'Arré! Who made this? Chole is my specialty. I always make it.'

'Padma, we are simple people. And your food has become a bit too *spicy* for us,' says Gunjan sarcastically.

'Better take your chole, Padma,' says Helma. 'No one is going to eat it.'

'I don't understand,' says Mrs Joshi, confused.

'How will you understand when there's so much going on in your house?' says Savita.

'Huh?' says Mrs Joshi, startled. *What do they know?* 'What do you mean? Nothing's going on in my house!'

'Really? Because we heard that—' says Helma.

Mrs Joshi blinks. She's scared. 'What?'

'Didn't your Mr tell you? His promotion has been given to that Mumbai-wallah, Sandeep Oberoi,' says Gunjan.

Mrs Joshi looks horrified and blurts out, 'What?'

'He's hiding things from you, and you're hiding things from us,' says Savita.

'Me? I'm not hiding anything,' says Mrs Joshi. She looks around, flustered. 'I don't understand what's going on.'

'Even we don't understand,' says Gunjan, 'whether to congratulate you or curse you.'

'You'll become a nani, but who will you say is the father at your grandchild's *naamkaran*?' says Helma.

Mrs Joshi steps back in shock.

'I must say you don't look so modern, Padma! Have you even been to Mumbai? Or do you think it's ok to suddenly start behaving like a city girl?' says Savita.

The three women laugh at Mrs Joshi.

'I must say, we certainly didn't expect this from Ladoo of all people. The *billi* has become a *sherni*!' says Helma.

'She's obviously influenced by the younger one,' says Gunjan.

'You should've spared a thought for *our* daughters, Padma,' says Savita. 'What message are your girls giving our girls? To get divorced? To roam around with white men at Café India? And now—shame, shame!—to have a child without marriage? What else is left for *your* daughters to do?'

'Nothing! What can be more shameful than *this*?' says Gunjan.

'That is why, in our times, girls were not sent to school or allowed to work,' says Helma. 'They were kept under check, like Padma's girls should have been.'

Kavya's voice interrupts their conversation, 'What's going on here? Why are you troubling my Padma Mausi?'

'She's not your Mausi,' says Helma.

'In my heart she is,' snaps Kavya. 'So, what are you doing?'

'We are doing nothing,' says Gunjan. 'We were telling Padma that if one daughter is out of control, we understand. But both daughters? Then the mother is only to blame, na?' Kavya glares at Gunjan, who quickly adds, 'I mean, I'm not saying it. People are.'

Mrs Joshi stumbles back and sinks into a chair in shock.

Kavya rushes to her. She hands Mrs Joshi a glass of water.

'Why are mothers blamed for everything the kids do wrong, and fathers praised for everything the kids do right? It's the kids who should be blamed or praised, no?' says Kavya angrily to the women. 'Especially in this case, when it's not Mausi's fault, but her daughter's fault.'

'Kavya, daughters are their mother's reflection,' says Savita. 'Anyway, we had told you to *not* invite Padma to your kitty party. Why is she here?'

'We are telling you clearly, Padma. You are out of our kitty . . . ' says Helma.

' . . . and our mandir WhatsApp group,' says Gunjan.

' . . . and don't come to our satsangs,' says Helma.

'We have unfriended you on Facebook as well,' says Savita. 'Forgive us, but we need to keep our daughters away from yours.'

A few women gather around them, friends and faces Mrs Joshi knows and loves.

Gunjan looks at them and says, 'Trust me, I feel bad because Padma was the most popular lady in our group. And now, I can't even repeat what people are saying about her!'

Mrs Joshi looks helplessly at Kavya and says, 'What's happening, beta? I can't believe I'm hearing all this.' She gets up, crying. 'How does everyone know my family's secret?'

No one says anything. Kavya shifts uncomfortably.

'You all can say and do what you want, but remember that today's modern generation thinks differently,' continues Mrs Joshi. 'You may think I have no respect left, but for Kavya's brother's wedding I am sitting at the pheras. I haven't lost my standing in society because of my daughters.'

Everyone stares at Kavya. Kavya looks shamefaced.

'Actually, errr, Mausi,' says Kavya.

'Yes, beta?'

'You see,' says Kavya slowly. She scratches her chin nervously. 'Because of all this, my mother called this morning. She said that my brother's in-laws are not . . . they will not be . . . err . . . comfortable if you come for the wedding. I'm sorry, Mausi. I can't do anything about this.'

Mrs Joshi looks like the Lakshman Jhula has fallen on her.

'Tell us something, Padma. Who is Ladoo's child's father? Is it that short fellow we keep seeing with her? Or that AIIMS chap Varun whom she's romancing?' asks Gunjan.

'I. Don't. Know,' says Mrs Joshi. This is all news to her. Who's Varun?

'How will she know?' says Helma. 'When her own daughter doesn't know who the child's father is!'

'Padma, your biggest mistake is that you let Ladoo come back from her husband's house. Daughters are *paraya dhan*. You should have broken her legs that time only and sent her packing to her in-laws. Then, none of this would have happened,' says Savita.

Mrs Joshi looks at the women for a long time. Then she wipes her tears and turns around to leave.

Kavya runs after Mrs Joshi, carrying her two chole dishes and shouting, 'Mausi, your food! Don't forget your food!'

Mrs Joshi enters her house. She sees Ladoo sitting with Bua, Tamara and Mr Joshi in the living room, merrily laughing away.

Mrs Joshi shouts, 'Did you get an abortion?'

Ladoo stands up in shock. 'What?'

'Did you do it or not? Yes or no? Yes or no?' Mrs Joshi walks up to Ladoo. 'Did you or not?'

Ladoo shakes her head.

'Tell me now!' screams Mrs Joshi.

'I'm not going to do it, Maa,' says Ladoo, meekly but firmly.

Mrs Joshi gives Ladoo a tight slap. Kavya starts in shock. What has she done?

The chole dishes fall from her hands and splatter on the ground.

14

A staff meeting is in progress at the Rishi Cash office. Inside a small conference room, amidst a lot of chitter-chatter, people are pitching editorial ideas. Ladoo is quiet and withdrawn.

'Ladoo?' asks Sanaya.

Ladoo snaps out of her thoughts and says, 'Hmmm?'

'Any new ideas? Something that can go viral? Something new or different?'

Ladoo looks down at her empty notepad and says, 'Errr . . . no.'

'What about unwed mothers?' Shazia makes a snarky comment. 'You know . . . having a baby, without having a daddy?'

Everyone sniggers. Ladoo looks up from her notepad in shock.

'Whaa—' she says.

'Chill, Ladoo,' says Sanaya. 'It's ok. Nothing to be embarrassed about. We're all cool.'

'Tots. I'm only worried about how Ladoo will continue the show with Gautam Sir now?' says Shazia in a fake sweet voice.

'What does her personal life have to do with our show?' asks 410, annoyed.

'Sir, sorry!' says Shazia. 'Don't mind. I didn't mean any offense. I'm not talking about Ladoo's scandalous pregnancy. I'm talking about the comments we have been getting online.'

Shazia holds up her phone. 410 looks at it. He turns away.

'Show them to me,' says Ladoo.

'Don't!' says 410.

But Shazia pushes her phone towards Ladoo. 410 grabs it.

'Why can't I see the comments?' asks Ladoo, snatching the phone from 410's hand.

'Because it's stupid. Childish, yaar. People say anything online. Especially about women. You should know more than me,' says 410.

Ladoo reads the comments.

Can't you get better-looking anchors?

We don't want Aunties on TV.

Someone get her a personal trainer.

Her arms are so big they're covering the little guy.

'Look, I don't want to comment on your personal life, Ladoo,' says Sanaya. 'But the ratings are dropping. Because of, you know—'

'Fine! Then remove me from the show,' says Ladoo angrily.

'What? That's not fine,' shouts 410. He looks at Sanaya and adds, 'What's this? You're a woman. You should support other women!'

'I agree, Sir!' says Shazia. 'We're small-town folk, but we're woke. We binge-watch Netflix and *Too Hot to Handle*. We don't care. But we'd love to know . . . who's the father, Ladoo?'

'Shazia,' warns 410.

'No, it's ok,' says Ladoo. She takes a deep breath. She knew this moment would come. 'There's no father. I've done IVF using a sperm donor.'

'Donor? Like *Vicky Donor* type?' says Shazia sarcastically. 'How modern of you. You are very bold to have a child like this.'

'But have you forgotten that this is India, babe?' another colleague, Rimjhim, says, in false concern. 'People will call you and your child all sorts of names. The B-word, the S-word, the C-word. I can't even imagine. That poor baby. You should've thought about all this before doing something rash. Yas?'

'She's right,' says Sanaya. 'This is not *sanskari*. It's not our *parampara*.'

Ladoo grips her notepad and feels the ceiling coming down on her. She gets up to go.

410 holds her hands and snaps back, 'What do you idiots know about India's sanskar and parampara? Do you know that Kunti gave birth to Karan without being married? That Sita was adopted? That Draupadi was born through surrogacy? Our shastras normalized

women having children as per their choice. Then, who are you to pass judgement? Who are you to make modern India more regressive than ancient India? Stop watching these Western shows. They don't make you progressive. Watch *Mahabharata* and *Ramayana* on Doordarshan. Change your outdated way of thinking. And, till then, shut up!'

There's a stunned silence in the room. Sanaya, Shazia and Rimjhim look aghast. Ladoo turns away from them. She is embarrassed. Then, she gets up and walks out of the conference room.

410 runs after her, shouting, 'Ladoo! Stop!'

Ladoo stops, but then hears a voice from the conference room say, 'Donor, my foot! 410 must have knocked her up and now they're trying to cover up. Remember *Maine Pyar Kiya*? *Ek ladka aur ladki kabhi dost nahin ho sakte*.'

'Seriously! Who do they think they're fooling?' another person says. 'He must be paying her to keep quiet about carrying his bastard child.'

Ladoo hears sniggers. She walks back into the conference room, in a huff, and says, 'It's actually none of your business, but this baby has a father and it's my boyfriend Varun. Ok? So quit gossiping like some loafers, and get back to pitching real ideas. Your careers need them.'

Ladoo walks out of the office to the main road.

410 runs after her, shouting, 'Ladoo, wait! Where are you going? Walk slowly, baba. You're pregnant!'

He tries to help Ladoo over a pothole, as he always has. But Ladoo pulls her hand away in anger.

'What the hell were you doing back there, 410?' Ladoo turns to look at him and asks. 'You can't fight with everybody in office. People are going to say things!'

'What?' says 410 in anger. 'I was the only one taking your side in there, Ladoo! You can't bend over and act spineless. You don't have to defend your life to anybody, but you have to own it! Speak up for yourself so I don't have to.'

'I have enough shit on my plate, 410! Why are you spoiling my office environment as well?' she snaps back.

'I can't believe you were ok with letting go of the show,' says 410 in frustration. 'We need to see pregnant women on camera. They shouldn't be forced to go into hiding. You should've insisted that they keep you.'

'I don't care about the show, 410.'

'But you do care about yourself, right? There comes a time in every woman's life where she must decide whether she's a Nirupa Roy or a Lalita Pawar. This is the time for you to be a Lalita Pawar. Stop acting like some bloody abla nari! If you weren't apologetic, no one would've had the guts to say anything to you. We would have been fine.'

'What is this we-we, 410? Are you the child's father? Are you pregnant?'

'Shhh! Someone will hear you, yaar!'

'Why are you doing this?' Ladoo asks 410. 'Why do you care so much?'

'What? I'm just being a friend.'

'No, 410. I've seen your friendship. You've never been this possessive about me. What's going on?'

410 looks at Ladoo for a long moment. He stops walking. He pulls her to a corner, where no one can see them. He bites his lips and says, 'I think . . . I don't know . . . how do I say this? I'm feeling something different.'

'What? I can't hear you. You're mumbling.'

410 raises his voice, 'Ladoo, I know I'm not the father of your child, but I am allowed to have feelings, right?'

'What feelings?' asks Ladoo suspiciously.

'I . . . I think I'm in *like* with you.'

'Eh?'

'I mean . . . I'm getting feelings for you which were not there before.'

'What feelings?' she asks.

'Love feelings. Like . . . romantic feelings.'

'What? Dude, this is not the time to be funny.'

410 looks at Ladoo earnestly. She reels back in shock.

'You're serious?' she says. 'What's wrong with you, man? My life is really complicated right now. I don't need this. I need my friend. Why are you creating more problems for me?'

'My feelings are *problems* for you?' says 410, hurt. 'I know you're pregnant, Ladoo, but everything is not always about you. It would be nice if you focused on my feelings once in a while.'

Ladoo takes a deep breath. He's right. 'I'm sorry,' she says. 'I didn't mean that.'

'I hope not. A guy just told you that he likes you and you called him a problem.'

'410, this is just not feeling real, ok? I'm sorry, but it's not,' says Ladoo. 'I'm seeing somebody. He's the biological father of my baby. I should be with him. Start a family with him. It's better for the child and for me.'

'Really? Have you even told Varun the truth?'

Ladoo shifts on her feet and says, 'I . . . will.'

'And how do you think he's going to respond?'

'I don't know.'

'You haven't told him,' says 410 slowly, 'because you know he's not going to be okay with this. Am I right?'

'Don't be an ass, 410.'

'Look, Ladoo. If you want to start a relationship with a lie, good luck! But a weak guy like Varun will *not* accept that you were shopping for sperm, even if it is his.'

'Shut up, 410,' says Ladoo, her voice thin.

'Why? Look, I'm telling you the truth. Varun is your Mr Right Donor. But he's not your Mr Right, ok? You have to accept that.'

'How dare you? What do you even know about relationships, 410? You're almost forty and you've never even had a serious relationship. How do you expect me to take you seriously?'

410 steps back in shock. His eyes tear up.

'What?' he says in disbelief.

'Come on, man!' says Ladoo. 'You don't like me. You're just doing this out of pity. I know you. And I don't need your handouts any more, ok? I can handle my own life.'

'Ok, Ladoo' says 410 softly. 'Whatever you say. You're always right, right?'

'410, come on! That's not what I mean.'

'I'm going to go. Good luck with everything.'

410 steps back into the street. Ladoo watches him walk away. He stumbles on the pothole that he has always saved her from. He falls. Ladoo reaches out but 410 quickly gets up. She sees him wipe a tear.

'Shit! I'm sorry, 410,' Ladoo shouts after him. 'I'm sorry!'

But 410 vanishes into the crowd. Ladoo kicks the ground. What has she done?

15

Ladoo is waiting outside AIIMS hospital. She plays with strands of her hair, nervously. She pats her stomach a few times. When she sees Varun come out of the building, she runs towards him.

'Varun! Hi!' she says. 'I've been trying to call you for days. You haven't called back?'

Varun looks at her coldly and says, 'What would I call and say, Ladoo? Where would I begin? That my girlfriend is pregnant? And she's told everyone that I am the kid's father?'

Ladoo takes a sharp breath and closes her eyes.

'Who told you?' she asks.

Varun walks towards his parked scooter. He gets on it.

'Someone called Shazia replied to my comment on your sister's some Insta post. I traced her and spoke to her.'

'I didn't know all this.'

'How would you know? You're never on social media. And, I'm sure, with her millions of comments, your sister wouldn't have even noticed mine.'

'I'm so sorry, Varun. I should've told you the truth.'

'I don't understand. Why are you telling everyone that I'm the father?' Varun looks around and whispers. 'Ladoo, we haven't even had sex!'

Varun starts his scooter.

'I'm sorry,' says Ladoo. 'I said it by mistake, ok? Please, Varun, give me a chance!'

Ladoo puts her hand on the scooter keys in the ignition.

'Mistake?' says Varun. 'This is not a mistake, Ladoo. It's a lie.'

'I didn't mean for all this to happen like this,' pleads Ladoo.

'It's not just this, Ladoo. You've lied about everything from the beginning. Everything about this relationship is a lie. Aren't you ashamed of yourself?'

'I am. A lot. But, Varun, my feelings for you are not a lie. They're real.'

'Real?' scoffs Varun. 'Nothing about you is real, Ladoo!'

'Look, I'm really sorry, Varun. But I've not lied. I am pregnant and you are the father! Believe me!'

'What? Have you lost it? You know you have to have sex to get pregnant, right?'

Ladoo sighs. 'Ok, please don't go. I'll tell you the truth. I used . . . your . . . donation . . . Bharosa Clinic . . . that's how I found you!'

'What?'

Varun looks around. He pulls Ladoo away from the scooter and towards the river.

He whispers urgently, 'How do you know that . . . err . . . donation is mine?'

Ladoo remembers her promise to Meera about not telling anyone how she got the donor's details.

'It doesn't matter,' she says.

'That's all that bloody matters!' shouts Varun. 'The donor's identity is supposed to be anonymous! It's on the contract I signed with them. I am going to sue that clinic. I'm going to make sure they shut down.'

'Wait! Please don't! It's not the fault of the clinic. I . . . I stole that file. I mean the donors' file. I did research on all the donors and selected you.'

'You mean to say our meeting was planned?' says Varun slowly. 'You told me that my name came up on Facebook as a "friend suggestion". That's why you sent me a friend request and we ended up meeting. My God, Ladoo, what's wrong with you? How much do you lie? You need help!'

'Ok, Varun. I said I'm sorry. But I am telling you the truth now,' pleads Ladoo. 'And let's not forget. You lied to me too. You never told me that you're a sperm donor.'

'That is different. I donate for time pass, to make some money on the side.'

'Money? You're a doctor at AIIMS! How much money do you need?'

'Don't question me when what you're doing is weird. And desperate. Getting pregnant using a donor! I thought only ugly psycho chicks did that!'

Ladoo reels back in shock. And, then, laughs in disbelief.

'Aside from being greedy, you realize what a big hypocrite you're being, Varun? You're judging others for doing openly the very thing you do secretly?'

'You know what, Ms Desperate?' says Varun sarcastically. 'This was a big mistake. I want nothing to do with you. In fact, I never want to see you again. Got it? Never.'

Varun turns to go.

Ladoo asks softly, 'What about our child, Varun?'

'*Our* child,' Varun scoffs. 'I'll have *my* child the old-fashioned way. With a wedding and a wife. Not with someone who is so . . . so . . .'

' . . . desperate?' says Ladoo softly.

Varun shakes his head in disgust. He walks off.

Ladoo stares at Varun's retreating figure for a minute. Then she turns around and stares at the Ganga. She wipes a tear and touches her belly as if to say, 'It will be okay.'

16

After an hour of staring at the river, Ladoo hails a rickshaw. On the way home, she can't stop her tears. To distract herself, she decides to see the comment that Shazia put up on Insta, which led to her relationship unravelling.

Ladoo logs into her Instagram account. She goes to her sister's account and scrolls through a few posts till she finds a photo of Tamara at Café India drinking a frappuccino with the hashtag: *#CoolingOff*. Ladoo goes through the comments section and finds Varun's comment: *#IWant*. Below that is Shazia's comment, in caps: *WANT THAT??? OR YOUR BABY MAMA???* with the sticker of a pregnant chick with a ladoo next to her.

'This Snarky Shazia! She's not an intern, but an illness!' Ladoo mumbles to herself.

She's about to log off, when she notices a video story of Tamara, doing an asana, while eating a vada pav. She laughs, till she reads the caption: *Mumbai, moving to your city soon . . . courtesy #MahaTalentAgency. Gonna rock it! #MovingToMumbai #DreamsDoComeTrue*.

Tammy has put up this post a few hours ago. Ladoo can't believe it.

'Tammy is going to Mumbai?' she asks herself in shock.

Ladoo calls Tamara.

Tamara answers after a few rings.

'Dids, come home fast,' she tells Ladoo.

'What? I can't hear you.'

Tamara shouts, 'Come. Home. Fast.'

'Tammy, I can't hear you. I just saw your post. Are you going to Mumbai?'

'Dids. I can't hear you. Come home fast. Mom and Pops are fighting about—'

Ladoo cannot hear Tamara.

'Why didn't you tell me that you're moving to Mumbai?' she continues. 'How can you, Tammy? I know you're selfish, but so much? You had promised to help me raise my child. And now? Are only your social media followers important to you? Not your own sister? How can you leave me alone for your stupid ambition? How can you break your promise?'

There is silence.

'Hello? Hello?' says Ladoo. She's frustrated. 'Hello? This stupid network! Tammy?'

Ladoo looks at her phone. She sighs and then begins to cry.

'Tammy, you can't even hear what your sister is trying to tell you. How will I live without you?'

'Dids?' says Tamara.

Ladoo wipes her tears.

In a stronger voice, she adds, 'Yes, Tammy. There was a network issue. You couldn't hear me.'

'No, Dids. I heard you. But I'm not selfish. I've always dreamt of going to Mumbai. I supported your dream of getting pregnant, can't you support my dream as well?'

'Dreams are not built on broken promises, Tammy. But I can't stop you, right? So, do what you have to. Maa had told me the truth . . . that all of you will leave me. I was stupid to think that you're not selfish any more. Good luck. I hope you'll be happy being Mumbai's rani.'

Ladoo cuts the call and cries.

Ten minutes later, the rickshaw pulls up in front of house number 111. Ladoo gets out and walks towards the gate. Tamara comes running out, towards Ladoo.

'Tammy, not now!' Ladoo says, wiping her tears, 'I'm still upset! Leave me alone!'

Ladoo stops in her path. Mrs Joshi is standing near the door with two packed suitcases. She's holding Billi, whose two puppies are running around her feet. Kavya is standing next to her.

'What? What's happening here?' Ladoo asks Tamara.

Tamara is unable to speak. She's hugging herself, her face red and swollen with tears, trembling. Ladoo walks towards her sister, in shock, when she hears her father's beseeching voice say, 'Padma, we have been married for forty years! We have not spent even one night apart since Ladoo was one!'

Ladoo looks in confusion at her father, as he turns to her and says, 'Now, because of you, Ladoo, your mother is leaving this house. Leaving me.'

'What?' Ladoo says and runs to her mother. 'Maa? Why? Why are you going? Where are you going? What is happening?'

Mrs Joshi ignores Ladoo. She puts Billi down, goes back to the house and begins to collect her belongings from the living room, tossing them angrily into a duffel bag. She stops to look at a photo of the family, hanging on the wall, scoffs at it and walks away.

'Beta, you had promised me that no one would find out,' Mr Joshi tells Ladoo. 'But everyone knows. How can I support you now?'

'Papa, I swear I didn't tell anyone,' says Ladoo. 'I don't know how word got out. But how does it even matter now? As long as we're all together, we will manage everything.'

'No, beta. I cannot manage anything now. See what chaos you've caused. You've destroyed our family because of your stupid mistake,' says Mr Joshi.

'Don't say anything to Ladoo, Bhaiya,' says Bua. 'She's pregnant. She needs love and happiness.'

'Exactly, Pops! This is all my fault. I was the one who told Dids to do all this. Scold me, not her,' says Tamara. She turns to her mother and, as fresh tears flow down her cheeks, she says, 'Maa, I will stop eating eggs. I will stop wearing short clothes. I will even leave social media.' She picks up her mother's suitcases. 'Please, don't leave.'

'Why are you telling Maa to stay, when you're the one who's leaving, Tammy?' says Ladoo. 'Have you told Maa about your big offer from Mumbai?'

Tamara looks guiltily at the floor.

'Tammy, you're so obsessed with social media that you don't know what's happening in real life. You should've informed us. Asked us. But no, you're on your own trip!' says Ladoo.

'Dids, I don't want to leave you,' says Tamara. 'But this is a fabulous opportunity for me. It'll help me become a mega influencer. Do web series and what not! I'm confused about what to do.'

'Don't be confused, Tammy,' Mrs Joshi's voice cuts into their conversation. 'And don't listen to your sister. She wants to take us all down with her. You've waited for this all your life. Take it. Go to Mumbai.'

'Maa, that's not fair,' says Ladoo. 'I always think of everyone's happiness.'

'Is that so? In that case, have you aborted this child?' says Mrs Joshi.

'No,' Ladoo looks sternly at her mother and says, 'And I'm eight weeks pregnant now, so never speak of this again.'

'An abortion can be done till twenty weeks,' says Kavya.

'What exactly is your problem, Kavya?' snaps Ladoo. 'Don't you have your own family to go ruin? Run to them. This is our private matter.'

Kavya replies, 'Mausi is my family. She's coming to stay with me.'

'Don't you have your *own* mother?' Ladoo asks Kavya. 'Then why are you after ours?' She turns to her mother, 'Maa, what is all this?'

'Everyone calm down,' says Bua. '*Shani* is going on. That's why all this is happening. It's no one's fault.'

Mrs Joshi ignores Bua, as usual, and continues, 'I'll come back home after you stop this madness you've started, Ladoo, and get rid of the baby. That's my condition. Once we put this whole thing behind us, you can start your life on a clean slate, and we can tell people that someone had spread a false rumour about this bastard child.'

'This child is not a bastard, Maa. This child is my baby,' Ladoo snaps angrily at her mother. 'If you're fond of killing babies, why didn't you kill me? At least I wouldn't have been cursed with a mother like you!'

'How dare you?' says Mrs Joshi. 'I am giving you one last chance. If you can't drop the child, then give it up for adoption! After that, we'll get you married and you can have as many children as you want. Ok?'

Ladoo starts crying, 'Maa, how can you even say that?'

'Why not? Rita is having kids at fifty!'

'Maa, I don't have Rita Aunty's fertility! This is my last chance to have my own child! Don't you understand that? Have you not heard a word I've said from the beginning?'

'Have you heard a word that I've said?' snaps her mother. 'You're ruining everything because of your stubbornness.'

'I'm not ruining anything,' says Ladoo. 'You are.'

'Fine, do what you want,' says Mrs Joshi. 'But you'll never have my blessings or support.'

'You know what? That's ok. Because I'm tired of trying to please everyone. I don't care any more if my child does not have a nani or a father or a masi. Because *my* child will have me! We are one. And if you love me, you'll have to love my child.'

'No one will love this bastard child,' Mrs Joshi says coldly.

Everyone gasps, even Kavya.

'Maa!' says Tamara, her voice quivering.

'It doesn't matter,' says Ladoo, her voice growing stronger. 'I will love my child, without conditions. Because I'm not my mother. I'm not you.'

Ladoo walks off in anger.

'*Badtameez*!' Mrs Joshi shouts after Ladoo. 'Every daughter is her mother! Don't ever forget that!'

Mrs Joshi lifts the half-empty duffel bag and walks out of the door, still shouting, 'I've cut my own stomach to raise you. I've been a good mother, a good wife and a good daughter-in-law, none of which you've been.'

Mr Joshi holds his wife and says, 'Don't leave us, Padma. Please! We will do whatever you say. I will go with you to the temple and satsangs. Mina will cook. Tammy will stop using her phone.'

'Will you tell your daughter to have an abortion?' asks Mrs Joshi.

Mr Joshi gasps in shock but says nothing.

'Even a thief is not scared of punishment, but of disrespect. Your Premchand said this, ji,' says Mrs Joshi. 'I will remember the disrespect you've shown me by taking Ladoo's side, even when she's wrong, even if you can't say it out loud!'

Mrs Joshi picks up Billi with her free hand and walks off. Kavya picks up Mrs Joshi's two suitcases and follows her.

Mr Joshi runs after Mrs Joshi, shouting, 'Birds that fly in the sky eventually return home. Premchand said this as well!'

But Mrs Joshi walks into Kavya's house, without even looking at him or at any of them.

Mr Joshi returns home alone and disheartened. Tamara clutches Billi's abandoned puppies and cries. Bua prays to Lord Shiva. Ladoo lies down on her bed, holding her stomach and wiping a tear. She feels the urge to throw up and runs into the bathroom.

The house turns dark, with no sound, except for soft cries.

17

Two months pass.

Ladoo is on the examination bed at Bharosa Fertility Clinic. Her sonography is underway.

The doctor asks her, concerned, 'No one has come with you, Ladoo?'

'No, I thought it's a routine sonography,' says Ladoo, shifting uncomfortably. 'Dr Ma'am, is everything ok? You've never taken this much time.'

The doctor looks at Nurse Asha and then points to the screen.

'Don't panic, Ladoo. But there's a reason I wish someone was with you today.'

'Dr Ma'am, what's wrong?'

'I'm seeing an echogenic focus in the foetal left heart. The cerebral diameter is also big. This is common in geriatric pregnancies. It's probably nothing. But, just to be safe, after four weeks, we'll take a closer look at the twenty-week anomaly scan and quadruple blood test. Ok?'

Ladoo panics, 'What exactly do you mean?'

'Relax, Ladoo. This is simply to rule out autism, Down's syndrome and chromosomal abnormality.'

'What? That sounds serious! Is the baby ok?'

'Yes. The foetus is fine. See its head, hands and feet. All is ok. But for the next few weeks, don't take any stress, walk thirty minutes every day and eat healthy. Your reports are showing that you're not happy. Be happy. For the sake of the child. Ok?'

'I will,' Ladoo nods and touches her belly.

'Take a deep breath,' says Nurse Asha kindly. 'Everything will be fine.'

Ladoo takes a couple of deep breaths and says, 'It's something to think about, Dr Ma'am. A child cannot be happy, even in the womb, if their mother is not happy. Maybe that's why they call childbirth and motherhood a miracle?'

Ladoo sighs wistfully and looks at her phone screensaver: a photo of her mother.

After the visit to the doctor, Ladoo decides to take it easy for a month. She wants to be left alone. Since 410 barely speaks to her and Shazia is now recording the show with him, Ladoo doesn't see the point of going to office. She files her articles from home. She lies in bed and reads, everything from the Gita—for her foetus's development—to *Cosmopolitan*—for hers. She watches Ramayana and Mahabharata, hoping that her foetus will imbibe the epics' lessons, and then binge-watches shows like *Sex and the City* on mute, so only she can hear it.

Her family members are as much in their own world. Tammy walks around in a daze, lying on the mirchi gadda most of the day, deleting all her social media posts, as she's not comfortable being online any more. Bua spends all day in the kitchen, teaching herself recipes from YouTube and not letting herself watch reruns of Big Boss. Mr Joshi goes to office and mopes about at home for the rest of the time, listening to his audiobooks in bed, his hand inadvertently reaching out for his absent wife.

In Kavya's house, Mrs Joshi is no better off. She looks unhappy, even though she's surrounded by Kavya's excited kids and an even more excited Kavya, pampering her with tasty food, the colony gossip and leg massages.

The only thing Ladoo finds the energy to do is to leave a box of fresh motichoor ladoos from Doon Halwai at Kavya's doorstep every Sunday. These are her mother's favourite. For the first few Sundays, the box is left untouched. But then it's not!

18

Ladoo is clutching the clinic's examination bed, softly chanting the Gayatri Mantra, as the doctor does her twenty-week anomaly scan.

'Dr Ma'am, I've thought about this,' she tells the doctor. 'Even if my child has a problem, mental or physical, I'll still give birth to it.'

'Why are you thinking such negative stuff, Ladoo?' asks Nurse Asha.

'I'm not. It's just when my Maa found out that she's having another girl, she decided to keep it. Like her, I'll never abandon my flesh and blood.'

'Your baby is fine,' says the doctor, pointing to the screen. 'See, the swelling has receded. The echogenic chamber is so small that it's negligible. Your blood reports are also clear. Congrats! Your baby is healthy and normal.'

Ladoo lets out a big sigh of relief. Finally, she smiles. Nurse Asha gives her a thumbs up.

Wiping a tear, Ladoo gets up from the table and says, 'Thank you, Dr Ma'am.'

'And see what a cheeky monkey he is—' adds the doctor, pointing to the foetus sticking its tongue out, '—like the mother.'

'*He*? It's . . . my baby is a boy?'

The doctor points to a sign that says, 'NO SEX DETERMINATION', and adds, 'Nice try!'

They laugh. Suddenly, Tamara and 410 barge in with Meera.

'Meera, you cannot let anyone into the examination room like this!' says the doctor sternly.

'I'm sorry,' says Meera, 'but I couldn't bear to see Ladoo alone any more! I had to call them!'

'And we are not *anyone*, Dr Ma'am. We are her family,' says 410.

'Really?' asks the doctor, mockingly. 'And how exactly are *you* related to Ladoo?'

'Errr . . . I'm the father of the child?' says 410, scratching his head.

The doctor looks at Ladoo and shakes her head, 'Looks like you're surrounded by cheeky monkeys.'

410 smiles and holds Ladoo's hand. They look at each other and grin.

'Friendship means no sorry, right?' says 410.

Ladoo nods.

'Dr Ma'am,' asks Tamara. 'Is that my nephew or niece on screen? So cute! Can I take a video, please? And 100 photos! It will not hurt the baby, right?'

'Of course not! The baby is sticking out its tongue again. Capture these moments!'

They all look and coo at the sonograph. Tamara begins to take videos and photos.

'Ladoo, the next scan is in four weeks,' says the doctor. 'Continue what you're doing. Enjoy yourself. You can even travel if you want.'

Ladoo smiles from ear to ear. She looks at Tamara and 410, and says, 'Did you hear that? I can travel! Yay!'

Tamara and 410 smile at her.

'Come on, enough of this *rona dhona*,' she adds. 'Let's go somewhere. How about Mussoorie? That's just two hours away. We can take 410's car. Can I, Dr Ma'am?'

'Of course! Travel while you can,' says the doctor. 'Trust me, you'll be stuck at home for a while after the baby comes.'

The doctor leaves.

'Good idea. Let's go to Mussoorie,' says 410. 'Anyway, my Scorpio was getting bored in the garage.'

He looks at Meera for effect.

Ladoo smiles indulgently and says, 'Meera, come with us. It'll be fun!'

'Really?' asks Meera. 'Are you sure? Ok!'

'What about your work?' asks Tamara.

'Who cares? Mom will not mind,' says Meera.

'Mom?' says 410. 'Nurse Asha?'

'No silly. The doctor.'

'The doctor is your mother? The one who called me a monkey?'

'Which you kinda are!' says Meera.

'Your mother owns and runs this clinic?' asks Tamara.

'Yes! Family business! Since forty years!' says Meera. 'You guys didn't know?'

'No!' says 410. 'How are we to know that the receptionist is the owner's daughter?'

'Oh, I'm doing admin work just to help Mom out. I'm actually a doctor. I just finished my last year of residency. I was going to join the practice, but our receptionist Mrs D'Souza left for Goa. It's tougher to find a good receptionist than to find a good doctor!'

'I knew it! When I first laid eyes on you—that day when I dragged Ladoo to the clinic—I knew we had found Rishikesh's best doctor,' says 410 flirtatiously.

'No, you didn't, 410!' Ladoo grins and says, 'Now, can you guys continue flirting in the car? I want to get to Mussoorie before sunset.'

19

Ladoo, Tamara, Meera and 410 are having a great time in the car.

They park on Mall Road, in Mussoorie, and walk around the shops. They take the cable car up to Gun Point. 410 and Meera run to a stall that has toy airguns to shoot balloons with. Ladoo and Tamara walk hand-in-hand and smile at each other.

'Babe,' says Ladoo to Tamara. 'I know I wasn't supportive earlier, but you belong in Mumbai. You have to go there, yaar. You'll rock it!'

'Dids, let's see,' says Tamara cagily.

'Just do what makes you happy, ok? Promise?' says Ladoo.

She hugs Tamara. Tamara smiles at her and almost trips on a rock.

'Be careful, Tammy,' warns Ladoo. 'You're so uncomfortable in this sari. Why have you worn it?'

'To impress Mom,' says Tamara. 'I want to show her that "Hot Yogini" has become "Sanskari Yogini". That you are a good influence on me.'

'That's very 1990s of you,' says Ladoo sarcastically. 'But how will Mom even see Sanskari Yogini, considering she refuses to look at us?'

'Dids, you know nothing!' says Tamara. 'You may not be on social media, but your mother is. She has an Insta account. Every day she likes my photos and videos.' Tamara opens her account and shows Ladoo a profile pic of an egg. 'See!'

'But this is an egg, an anonymous account? How do you know it's Mom?'

'Dids! See the pics! Only motichoor ladoos, that too from Doon Halwai. These are the ones that *you* leave for Mom every week.'

Ladoo looks closely. Tamara is right!

'Jai Bholenath! Even my mother is active on social media, and I'm not! This is embarrassing. I tell you what, Tammy, open my account as well!'

'Don't you have an account already?'

'I mean a new account. A professional one that captures my journey. The pregnancy, donor baby, single mom, *besharami* and scandal!'

'What? Dids, you . . . *you* want to go public? With your pregnancy?' asks Tamara, stunned. 'You? We were keeping it low-key, na?'

'We were. But that didn't happen now, did it?' says Ladoo. She smiles. 'But it made me realize that, if I don't own my life and be proud of my decisions, then nobody else will! My story matters. To me and to others. It's easy for women to think that they're alone in motherhood. It shouldn't be that way. We are in this together. And, for that, we need conversations. Because even if my journey is different today, talking about it will make it normal tomorrow. I have to do it! For all the women out there! For my kiddo!'

Tamara smiles indulgently at Ladoo, 'I love the idea! Let's do it!'

Tamara types something on her phone and asks, 'What should be the handle name?'

'I don't know!' says Ladoo sadly. 'Everyone's calling me a loose character . . . immoral . . . scandalous . . . *badnam*. They don't know that I've only had sex with one guy my entire life! I'm practically a virgin!'

Tamara chuckles, 'Should I put that down? The pregnant virgin?'

Ladoo cracks up, 'You na, Tammy! You make me laugh at the funniest moments.'

'Ok. What about: Geriatric Pregnancy? Budhi Amma? Thanda Anda?'

They both start laughing.

'How about Badnam Ladoo?' says Ladoo, finally. 'It's apt na?'

'Yas! It's lit!' says Tamara. 'Let's use it.'

Tamara high-fives her sister and types on her phone.

'Account created! Profile pic done. Now to post something,' says Tamara. 'What do you want as your first post?'

Ladoo looks at the picturesque view before her. The Doon valley, the Himalayas, the sprawling town below and the blue skies above. She sees a woman who is holding her fascinated young child and pointing out the Pithwara, Gangotri and Bandarpunch mountain ranges.

Our stories are all that matter.

'Let's make a live video!' says Ladoo slowly.

'You? Live video?' asks Tamara. 'What will you say?'

'Everything that I've been feeling for the past few months. I want my account to be honest, not rehearsed.'

'Ok, but we need someone to watch it and you have no followers. Let's do the video on my account, so I can cross-post and you can get new followers!'

'Ok, makes sense, Hot Yogini,' says Ladoo. She smoothens her hair and clears her throat, 'Ready? Let's do this!'

Tamara begins recording and says excitedly, 'Ok, you're live on Insta!'

Ladoo looks straight at the phone and says, 'Hi! My name is Amara Joshi. I'm a thirty-five-year-old divorcee from Rishikesh. My friends call me Ladoo. Last year, I decided to have a baby, using a sperm donor. When people in my small town found out, I became Badnam Ladoo. My Maa left our house. My Papa doesn't speak to me any more. My boyfriend dumped me. I lost a key position in my office.' She pauses and takes a deep breath. 'But today, I am five months pregnant. In my twenty-week anomaly scan, that is as scary as it sounds, my naughty baby stuck out its tongue like a monkey. It was having fun at a time I was freaking out.' Ladoo laughs. 'My little kishmish made me realize that taboos are not real, nor are social sanctions. The only thing that's real is our fear of things. So, for the first time in my life today, I let go of my fears: of scandal, of pleasing people, of being perfect, of controlling things, of being a single mother, and even of—as you can see—social media. Today I realized that to be a mother, a woman can go from being Nirupa Roy to Lalita Pawar, from an abla nari to a krantikaari. Because those who do things differently are not outrageous but courageous! So, here's to our hatke tribe! May we keep growing!'

Tamara stops recording.

'Dids, that was legit! Slayed it!' she says and claps.

Meera and 410 walk up to them.

'What are you doing?' Meera asks Tamara.

'I think the roadside truck is trying to become a family Maruti,' jokes 410, peering at the video. 'New and improved version.'

Ladoo smacks him on the back. He laughs.

'You look amazing in this, Ladoo,' says Meera.

'I didn't even need a filter or app,' says Tamara, 'thanks to this gorgeous background.'

'FML! No filter? No BeautyPlus?' says Meera excitedly. 'It's been so long since I've taken an unfiltered photo that I've forgotten what I look like IRL! Come na, Tammy. Let's take tons of photos! Selfies from Gun Point, with us holding guns?'

Meera runs towards the stall with the toy airguns. Tamara hobbles behind her.

'Hurry, babe!' complains Meera. 'Why the hell have you worn a sari with such high heels?'

'Don't you know? I'm a very *bad* feminist,' replies Tamara.

Ladoo laughs on hearing them.

'There you go,' she says. 'Shakuni Mama has found his Kansa Mama. Now we will see Ramayana's Mahabharat.'

410 grins.

He turns to her and says, 'Listen, Ladoo!' He pauses uncomfortably, 'We're cool, na?'

'Yes! Come, let me buy you coffee.'

410 and Ladoo walk to a nearby kiosk.

'One black coffee for my friend,' says Ladoo to the owner. 'And one mango milkshake for me, with extra cream!'

410 raises his eyebrows and asks, 'Your permanent diet is finally over?'

'Yes,' says Ladoo happily. 'I'm only going to enjoy life from now on. Anyway, with my collective sins, I'll be reborn as a cockroach in my next life. What's the point of being good any more?'

They laugh and cheer.

'Look,' says Ladoo. 'I know we didn't finish talking that day. And I'm sorry about that. But, 410, do you seriously think that we'll make a good couple?'

410 shrugs, 'I don't know, yaar.'

'I think we both know that there's only one way to find out. Kiss me!' says Ladoo.

'What?'

'Come on! Kiss me! That's the only way to know whether we have chemistry or not.'

'Jai Bholenath!' says 410, shifting uncomfortably on his feet. 'I don't know.'

'Do you have a better idea?' asks Ladoo. 'Like sex?'

'Yuck, no,' says 410.

Ladoo smiles cheekily at him. She has him cornered. 'Fine,' says 410 reluctantly.

Ladoo leans slowly towards 410's lips. 410 shuts his eyes and leans forward. Their lips touch.

They both quickly pull away. Both of them make a face.

'Nooooooo!' says Ladoo.

410 adds, 'This is not happening, yaar!'

Ladoo and 410 together shout, 'No way!'

'I knew it!' Ladoo laughs and says, 'I knew that the feelings you were having were not for me, but for your biological clock. Tick-tick-tick-tick-tick-tick, boss! You are ready to be a father!'

'Really?'

'Really, sweetie. I think we both know I'm not the right girl for you. Someone else is.' She nods towards Meera. 'Trust your heart, not your head.'

'Where does that leave us?' 410 asks Ladoo.

'I'm glad you asked. Because, 410, I have something to ask you.'

Ladoo goes down on one knee.

'M . . . marriage?' 410 panics and says, 'You want to marry me? Did you not see that we have no chemistry? Do you want another sexless marriage?'

'410, I love you!' Ladoo laughs and says, 'But as a brother. A friend. You're my buddy. I want you in my life forever. I want you to help me raise my child.'

410 chuckles in relief and says, 'What?'

'410, do you take me, your bestest friend in the world, as your co-parenting wife, without marriage, without sex, till death do us part?' says Ladoo.

'What?' asks 410, confused.

'Do you?'

'Yes! Yes! A 1000 times yes!' says 410.

He lifts Ladoo up, with some effort, and hugs her.

'I will always be there for you and that little monster that's sure to come out of you,' he says. He winks at Ladoo.

'With your upbringing, I'm sure the kid will be a monster!' says Ladoo and glares.

'Jokes aside, Ladoo. I am feeling so happy today,' says 410. 'Such a big weight has been lifted off me. My best friend is back in my life. I have a cute baby on the way. I fired that horrible Shazia, so we never have to see her again.'

'Finally!' says Ladoo.

'I feel like my heart is flying in this beautiful place. All that's missing is—'

'Please don't say—' says Ladoo.

'—a song—' Ladoo and 410 say together.

'410, no! You have a terrible voice!' adds Ladoo.

410 doesn't pay her attention and begins to sing, '*Yeh haseen wadiyan . . .*'

Behind him comes another voice, '*Yeh khula aasman . . .*'

It is Meera.

410 and Meera sing together, '*Aa gaye hum kahan . . . mere sajna . . .*'

They look at each other and laugh.

Ladoo and Tamara look at them and giggle knowingly.

'Looks like our 410 has found his 411,' says Ladoo with affection.

Tamara smiles and adds, 'Seriously! They're a match made in heaven.'

She turns to her sister. 'Dids, should we go now? The sun is about to set. Baby must be tired.'

'Look at you, already a concerned masi!' Ladoo teases Tamara.

They begin to walk back towards the cable cars. They stop at the ticket counter.

'Bhaiya, is there a special car for pregnant ladies?' Ladoo asks the ticket collector.

The ticket collector looks confused and says, 'But Madam, you're not pregnant.'

Ladoo laughs and says, 'Huh? Of course I'm pregnant. See my tummy, Bhaiya!'

The man scratches his forehead. He's unconvinced.

She looks at Tamara. 'Unbelievable. When I was *not* pregnant, everyone thought that I *was* pregnant. Now that I *am* pregnant, everyone thinks I'm *not* pregnant.'

'You better start wearing tight clothes from tomorrow, or everyone will think we made up this scandal,' says Tamara.

'Tammy! You also, na!' says Ladoo and laughs.

Ladoo takes out money to pay for the tickets when a thought hits her, 'One second. Meera, if you're the owner of Bharosa Clinic, then why did you take all those bribes from us?'

Meera giggles nervously and says, 'Oh that? That was just time pass! To give the clinic authentic feels . . . like receptionist feels?'

Ladoo glares at Meera.

'Are you Gujarati, Meera?' 410 asks her eagerly. He looks impressed.

'No, but don't I behave like one?' says Meera and grins.

410 nods. He sees Ladoo's disapproving expression and stops grinning.

Slightly jealous, Meera asks, 'By the way, where did both of you meet?'

'Ladoo was my junior in school, my junior in college, and now she's my junior in office!' says 410.

'But, in life, I've always been his senior. And you're treating us all to dinner, our darling non-Gujju Gujarati!' Ladoo tells Meera.

They laugh. They step into the car. 410 starts showing videos of his show 'Rishi Cash' to Meera who oohs and aahs, much to his delight. Tamara takes selfies of Ladoo and her. As Ladoo zooms into one photo, she sees something. She turns around in surprise. She points to a cable car that is approaching them.

'That trolley. Look at it, Tammy. Isn't that Sandeep there?'

Tamara turns to look. Ladoo is right. Sandeep Oberoi is inside the car, passionately kissing a woman. He suddenly looks up and sees them. His eyes become big. He pulls away. The woman he is kissing looks up. She turns around just as their cars are bang opposite each other. All four of them lock eyes.

Ladoo and Tamara's mouths open as they realize that the woman Sandeep Oberoi is kissing is Kamini Kavya!

20

It's dark inside Ladoo's house. Bua is in the kitchen cooking something. It's burning. Mr Joshi is standing on the terrace. He is hiding behind the clothes. He peeks through a dupatta to look at his wife who is on Kavya's terrace, staring out at the moon. She doesn't see him.

After a while, she goes down. Mr Joshi also goes down, trying to guess which room his wife is in. He goes from one room to another. He looks at Kavya's hall. Yes, Mrs Joshi is there! She is saying something to Kavya's children. Then she moves into the kitchen. Mr Joshi cannot see her. He gets frustrated. He goes into his kitchen.

'Mina! What are you burning now?' Mr Joshi asks his sister.

'Bhaiya, I was trying to make gajar halwa for Ladoo. But I cannot do all this! Bhabhi used to be the best cook. How will I ever cook like her?'

'Who do you think taught your *bhabhi* how to cook?' says Mr Joshi.

'Help me, then!' Bua tells her brother.

'No way,' says Mr Joshi. 'I am on another mission right now.'

He walks out.

'You're not helping me because I'm cooking this for Ladoo,' Bua shouts, so he can hear her. 'It's not good to be angry with your own daughter, Bhaiya. She's pregnant. We must be happy around her, so our grandchild comes out smiling.'

'Babies don't smile,' Mr Joshi shouts back. 'They pass gas, and we mistake it for smiling.'

Bua shakes her head in irritation.

Mr Joshi spots Mrs Joshi again. He doesn't want her to know that he's stalking her like this. He goes quiet and hides.

Bua shouts from the kitchen, 'Tammy called. They'll be back from Mussoorie in one hour or so. They had a great time there. We should also go. It's been so long.'

But Mr Joshi is not listening. He follows Mrs Joshi into the guest room in Kavya's house, which is Ladoo's room in their house. From Ladoo's window he watches as his wife takes out a blanket. He watches her drink a glass of water. He watches her comb her hair.

He sends her a WhatsApp message, 'ILU'. He sees her look at the message and then keep her phone down. She's still angry with him. Shit.

She goes into the bathroom to change.

At that moment, Mr Joshi's phone pings. Tamara has sent him a WhatsApp message. He opens it. For a second, he's not sure what he's looking at. He leans against the wall and looks more closely at the video. It's the sonography video of his grandchild. He puts his hand against his mouth, as he sees the baby swimming inside Ladoo's tummy. And, then, the baby sticks out its tongue. Mr Joshi gasps and chuckles. He wipes a tear brimming in his eyes.

He hears Mrs Joshi come out of the bathroom. She turns off the light. A glow comes on. She has turned on her phone. He hears words from the audiobook *Beti Ka Dhan*! Mrs Joshi is listening to Premchand, her husband's favourite author. Mr Joshi smiles.

Mr Joshi looks around Ladoo's room. It's dark. He turns on the light. He sees a baby cot, diapers and little onesies. He sees Ladoo's prenatal medicines, her books on pregnancy and motherhood, her vision board with photos of her many pregnancy scans and cute baby photos. There's a photo of their family on the board too. Mr Joshi runs his hands over this photo and then over his grandchild's scans. He realizes what a fool he's been. He begins to sob gently. He sits down on Ladoo's bed.

'I'm sorry, beta,' he says. 'How could I have left you alone at a time like this?'

He wipes his tears and takes a few deep breaths.

After a minute, Mr Joshi gets up and goes to the kitchen.

'Step aside, Mina,' he tells Bua. 'From now on I'm going to cook for my Ladoo.'

Bua smiles and says, 'Thank God! I can't eat burnt food any more.'

An hour later, when Mr Joshi hears the girls' voices, he takes a spoonful of halwa in a bowl and runs out. He waits till Ladoo reaches the front door and smiles at her. She seems surprised to see him there.

'Beta,' Mr Joshi says, 'I want you to taste your Papa's halwa. It's better than even your mother's halwa.'

Ladoo takes a bite. She nods in delight.

'It's true,' she says, 'that fathers are the world's greatest chefs.'

Mr Joshi and Ladoo hug.

'From now on,' he tells her, 'I'll take care of your prenatal medicines, diet, reports, doctor appointments and baby shopping. You just chill. I want my grandbaby to come out smiling.'

'Papa,' says Ladoo softly.

'Let me make up for what I did, beta,' says Mr Joshi. He wipes a tear. Ladoo squeezes his hands. 'By the way, what did you get me from Mussoorie?'

'Landor Bakehouse's chocolate cake. Your favourite. And motichoor ladoos for Maa.'

'Her favourite,' he says wistfully.

Ladoo gives the ladoo box to Tamara, who runs and keeps it at Kavya's doorstep.

'Great. We'll eat the cake after dinner,' says Mr Joshi. 'By the way, do you know that I'm going to be a nana soon?'

'Papa, you're really a tube light!' says Ladoo.

They walk into the house, laughing.

21

One evening, as Ladoo is returning home from work, Tamara comes running to the gate, shouting, 'Guess who's come home, Dids? That too with a million gifts? You will ROFWL.'

Ladoo walks into the house inquisitively. She sees Kavya, surrounded by many gifts.

'Errr, hi, Ladoo!' says Kavya awkwardly. 'I just came in. I guessed you'd be home by now.' Ladoo looks at her, confused. 'I brought some gifts for the baby. I hope you like them!'

'Wow, thanks, Kavya,' says Ladoo. 'But this is too much!'

'Yup!' says Kavya enthusiastically. 'I got almost everything that you'll need for a newborn baby!'

'But these gifts will not even fit in my room!'

'We'll make them fit,' Mr Joshi butts in impatiently. 'Kavya, how's their mother? Is she eating properly? Sleeping well? I hope she's taking her BP medicine?'

'She's fine, Uncle. She's comfortable, like at home. She's mixed well with my kids.'

They all look at each other awkwardly.

'Does she miss us?' Mr Joshi asks slowly.

'She's still angry,' says Kavya slowly, 'but she organized a havan in my house to make Ladoo less . . . errr . . . badnam. In fact, sometimes she even calls me Ladoo instead of Kavya. She's obviously missing all of you.'

Everyone looks at Ladoo, who looks down at the floor sadly.

'Kavya beta,' says Bua. 'Every night at 10 p.m., in Bhabhi's memory, I turn on Big Boss at full volume. Can Bhabhi hear it?'

'Yes, Aunty,' says Kavya sarcastically. 'I think the whole colony can hear it.'

'Good,' says Bua, not taking the bait. She lifts an automatic breast pump and asks, 'By the way, what is this?'

Tamara puts the pump on a toy doll's bum and says, 'Must be to suck out the baby's poop.'

Kavya turns to Ladoo and says, 'I don't think they know what's going to hit them!'

'Kavya,' says Tamara. 'Why are you here? And why have you suddenly turned from no-child to pro-child?'

Kavya shifts on the sofa and says, 'Because I understand Ladoo's need to have a child. Trust me, I've never loved anybody the way I love my children. Even when they irritate me, or exhaust me, they still make me happier than anything else in the world.' She turns to Ladoo. 'You're doing the right thing, Ladoo. A woman should have a child as per her wish and her convenience. Your body, your choice.'

'Wow, Kavya!' says Tamara. 'You should teach a course on how to turn from Pakistan to India.'

'Tammy!' warns Ladoo.

'It's ok, Ladoo,' says Kavya, distressed. 'Errr . . . can we speak in private? Please!'

'Ok,' says Ladoo.

She gets up and begins walking to her room. Kavya and Tamara follow her.

Outside the bedroom door, Kavya turns to Tamara and says, 'Actually, I want to talk to Ladoo alone.'

'No way, Kamini Kavya,' says Tamara.

'Excuse me? Did you just call me *kamini*?' asks Kavya.

'No!' Ladoo says quickly. 'She said mini. Mini Kavya. Because you're so thin.'

Ladoo glares at Tamara, but her sister continues, 'I'm not leaving you alone with Dids, ok? Say what you want in front of me. We both know why you're suddenly being sweet.'

'You told her about Mussoorie, Ladoo?' says Kavya, in distress.

'We *both* saw you that day, Kavya,' says Ladoo. 'Tammy was right next to me.'

'No, she wasn't,' says Kavya. 'The girl next to you was wearing a sari!'

'That was *me*!' says Tamara.

Kavya looks unconvinced as she says, 'I guess I didn't recognize Tamara with her clothes *on*!'

Tamara looks like she'll hit Kavya. Ladoo indicates to Tamara to come in and calm down. Ladoo shuts her room door. Kavya sits on Ladoo's bed, while Tamara chooses to stand, glaring at Kavya.

'Say what you want in front of Tammy,' Ladoo tells Kavya.

'Fine,' says Kavya. 'I came to say thank you for not telling anyone what you saw.'

'How do you know I didn't tell anyone?' asks Ladoo.

'It's a small town. If you'd told even one person, then everyone would've found out. Thanks for keeping my secret a secret.'

'*And* saving your ass. *And* your reputation. *And* your marriage,' Tamara chimes in.

'Tammy!' says Ladoo.

She turns to Kavya and says gently, 'It's ok. I don't believe in revenge.'

Kavya turns shamefaced and asks, 'How do you know?'

'Who else could it have been, Kavya?' says Ladoo. 'Who else hates me so much? But, trust me, it was a blessing that everyone found out my secret!'

'I'm so sorry, Ladoo!' says Kavya. 'Believe me, I'm not a bad person. I had a stupid fling, since Sandeep's marriage is kaput, and I'm struggling with mine. But our fling is over. He called it off after Mussoorie.'

'Hold on!' Tamara butts in. 'One second! Shirtless Sandy is getting divorced? Why?'

Kavya shifts uncomfortably and says, 'He told me I could tell you, because he trusts both of you. But, please don't tell anyone.' She pauses. 'Sandy wants kids. His wife doesn't. He tried to ignore his feelings for many years, but then his father got sick, very sick. Sandy began to rethink what he wanted from life. And a child is something he really wants.'

'That's great news!' says Tamara. 'So, tell me, when will his divorce be finalized?'

'Tammy!' says Ladoo.

'Look,' says Kavya. 'It wasn't easy for me to come here today. You know I *don't* like both of you. I mean *didn't*.'

'But why, Kavya? What have we ever done to you?' asks Ladoo.

'I guess . . . I don't know . . . maybe I was jealous!' Kavya replies softly.

'Eh?' says Ladoo in surprise. 'You? Jealous of us? How is that even possible?'

'What would you even be jealous of?' asks Tamara, equally surprised.

'You're so perfect! We are jealous of you!' says Ladoo.

Kavya shifts on the bed. She looks down at her nails and says softly, 'Look, I've always checked all the boxes and followed all the rules. My life is a template. I never had an option, did I? I got married to Dilip at twenty-three. I had kids before twenty-seven. I did whatever my mother told me to do. Whatever my husband told me to do. But you two? You were like free birds, doing whatever you wanted. Nothing was normal with you sisters. From not wearing appropriate clothes, to not remaining in a marriage, to having kids also differently. And Mausi is so nice. She never held you back. I wish I had a mother like that. I wish I could burn this rulebook that runs my life.'

'Is that why you're trying to steal our mother?' says Tamara.

'Not steal,' Kavya looks up at the ceiling sheepishly and says, 'But I think it's safe to say that she does deserve better.'

She chuckles.

'Kaminiiiii—' Tamara begins.

'Tammy!' says Ladoo. She turns to Kavya and adds, 'Sorry, but you are kind of kamini.'

Kavya sighs and says, 'I know!'

'And, you were having an extramarital affair! How exactly is that following the "rulebook"?' asks Tamara.

Kavya sighs and says, 'Do you have any idea how difficult it is to be this perfect? To look like this? Of course you don't!'

Tamara and Ladoo glare at her.

'What I mean is—' Kavya adds quickly, '—that first my mother counted my calories. Now my husband does. I basically married my mother! I am nothing to Dilip but a trophy wife, who must obey his commands and live by a fixed plan.'

'That must be tough,' says Ladoo.

'It is. And it's sooooo boring!' says Kavya. 'But, I finally spoke to Dilip about this. I told him I'll leave him, if he doesn't love me the way I deserve. Now we're working things out. He comes back from office early now. He talks to me. He pays attention to my feelings. He buys me ice-cream instead of dumbbells. I don't know if he's doing all this because he thinks a divorce will ruin our perfect image, or if he's genuinely changed. But, at least, we're finally happy.'

'Good. I'm glad,' says Ladoo.

'And you're lucky, Ladoo. You made the right decision. Trust me, very few husbands are good fathers. Most men think their contribution is over after giving one good sperm. That's why, when it comes to raising a child, it makes little difference whether or not you have a husband. The mother is enough,' says Kavya. She smiles and adds gently, 'And, you have your family. They are clueless, but they will be amazing parents.'

Ladoo and Tamara look at Kavya, and—for the first time—give her a genuine smile.

Kavya gets up from the bed and says, 'Again, sorry I was such a kamini. From now on I'll do my best and try to be a friend. A good friend!'

'Prove it by fixing Dids up with Sandy, since he's single and all!' says Tamara.

'Oh!' says Kavya, patting Tamara's face. 'To be young and foolish again!'

Tamara immediately gets angry and says, 'I told you Dids, she's not a woman, but a—'

'Tammmmyyyyy,' warns Ladoo.

Tamara grits her teeth and adds, '—but a superwoman. See you later, Kamini Kavya!'

images or ideas seemingly changed but, at last, as [illegible] finally happy.

"Could I explain," says Bullet.

[illegible]

[illegible]

Karan [illegible] and says. [illegible]

[illegible]

[illegible]

22

Tamara and Ladoo are alone, enjoying their kahwa at Café India.

'Dids,' says Tamara. 'I brought you here to tell you that I'm not moving to Mumbai.'

'What?' says Ladoo, putting her cup down. 'But why?'

'In Mumbai, you'll find a social media influencer every time you throw a stone. In Rishikesh, that stone will have to be hurled really, really far,' says Tamara. 'Rishikesh needs me more than Mumbai does.'

'Tammy, come on. Wasn't this your dream?' says Ladoo, tearing up. 'Tell me the truth.'

'The truth is that I have a new dream,' says Tamara. 'To be here with you, with my nephew or niece.'

'You're sacrificing your career for the sake of kids? That's such a stereotype! And it makes you such a—'

'—bad feminist!' sighs Tamara. 'I know. But I'm ready for this. You know why? Because when I went shopping today, I didn't buy anything for myself. I used my money to buy this.' Tamara holds up a onesie. 'How tiny are babies? And how can something so tiny be scary?'

'Ahem. You sound like *you* want a baby now?' Ladoo asks her sister, with a smile.

'Maybe. But, I still don't want a husband. So, I was thinking—inspired by you, of course—that maybe I'll freeze my eggs. Remember, Dr Ma'am had once mentioned that I'm at the right age. This way, I can have a baby on my own terms, when I want, the way my Dids has!'

Ladoo folds her hands in prayer and imitates Mrs Joshi, 'Thank God my daughter is no longer a lesbian . . . I mean Lebanese!'

Tamara laughs and then says, 'I miss Mom.'

'Me too.'

Just then an American walks up to them. He's with an angry-looking girl.

'Excuse me?' he says. 'But are you that Insta influencer—'

'One frappuccino—' says Tamara, on cue.

'—who is advocating sperm donation? Bad-nam La-doo?'

Tamara puts her head in her hands and laughs. Ladoo nods.

'Great!' says the American. 'I want you to know that my sister, and all her friends, love your work! My sister is in her forties. She was looking after our sick parents and, before she knew it, it was too late. Now, inspired by you, she's using a donor. As a thank you, can I buy you coffee? And get a selfie?'

'I can buy my own coffee, thanks. But a selfie is fine,' says Ladoo. She smiles softly as the man takes a selfie.

The angry-looking girl glares at Ladoo and says, 'Just to let you know, I'm not a fan. In fact, I think you're fake!

I don't want to get pregnant or have kids. I don't think every woman should be a walking womb. Why should I have to listen to your nonsense about fertility and babies? It's so redundant.'

Ladoo raises her eyebrows in amusement and says, 'Chill yaar! I don't expect everyone to like me or agree with me. And, I definitely don't think every woman is a walking womb. Becoming a mother should be an emotional decision, not a biological one. But, can I say one small thing? Even if you don't want to have kids, you must know about fertility. Every woman must. After all, it's our body. We should make the rules about it, but using knowledge, not hashtags.'

The girl nods, holds up a peace sign, and walks away.

'Dids, I'm sooooo proud of you,' says Tamara. 'You should give lessons on how to deal with a real-life troll. You're getting more fans and messages than I ever got! So many invites for events and endorsements! That's why I think we should do stem cell preservation for our baby, by cutting an endorsement deal with one of those stem-cell companies. Free preservation without reservation!'

'You're so extra, Tammy!' says Ladoo and laughs.

'I'm serious. Make hay while the sun shines. Because, you never know when the eclipse starts!' says Tamara.

A random guy walks up to them and says, 'Hi! Ladoo? I'm Vikas.'

Ladoo looks tired and says, 'Hi Vikas. We have enough to drink, thanks!'

'Err. Actually, I saw you on Tinder. Thought I'd say hi.'

'Tinder? I deleted that app from my phone like a year ago.'

'Oh! You must have deleted the app from your phone, without deleting the profile!'

'What? Jai Bholenath! I'm still on these dating apps? My thumb almost got fractured swiping on them!' says Ladoo. 'Sorry, but I'm not interested!'

'No worries, buddy. Let me buy you a samosa or bhatura or something.'

Ladoo frowns and then slowly gets up from her chair. 'Actually, *buddy*, how about buying me samosa and bhatura and burger and pizza, because you see . . . I'm pregnant.'

The guy looks at Ladoo's belly and scuttles off.

Ladoo chuckles, 'He's running like I have the corona virus!'

'Dids,' says Tamara. 'I never thought you'd reject a guy like this.'

Ladoo sips her chai and says, 'Babe, that's because I'm no longer desperate for a man's love. I'm happy being single!'

'Really? You sound like me!'

'I do. Because, like you, I've realized that being single does not mean being lonely. I'm enjoying my own company. I finally love myself! Is there a greater joy than that?'

'No, there isn't!' Tamara says and cheers. Both of them laugh.

'Now listen, Tammy,' says Ladoo. 'I was thinking that since I'm now infamous for something worse than divorce, I deserve a baby shower! It will be like my Filmfare where, after years of being nominated, I finally win an award. What say?'

Tamara nods excitedly.

And so, Kavya and Tamara throw a desi baby shower for Ladoo. They don't let her play the games, so that other people can win. They give her an award for being the 'Most Hatke Mother-To-Be'. They gift her a post-delivery bungee jumping lesson, so she can tick that off her bucket list. Surrounded by love, Ladoo has a blast! She is the happiest she's ever been in her life.

her years of being a mother, I finally [illegible] award. What [illegible]

I'm amazed [illegible].

And so [illegible] Famous [illegible] for [illegible] they [illegible] her [illegible] other people [illegible] [illegible] Mother Te[illegible] The [illegible] [illegible] [illegible] [illegible] [illegible] the [illegible] [illegible].

23

And then comes the labour. Ladoo is at AIIMS hospital, screaming in pain. The nurses are running around her, getting drips and medicines. 410, Tamara, Bua and Mr Joshi are by her side, looking frazzled and concerned.

'Maa! Maa! Maa!' shouts Ladoo, yearning for her mother, as women do in times of pain. 'Where is Maa?'

'Beta,' says Bua, massaging Ladoo's legs. 'Pay attention here. Focus on the baby. The pain will be over soon.'

Mr Joshi looks traumatized.

'I cannot watch my daughter like this. Excuse me,' he says.

Mr Joshi goes out of the room, as Ladoo screams more loudly.

The doctor turns to 410 and says, 'You don't look ok. Why don't you also step outside? Anyway, only two people are allowed in the labour room.'

'Me?' says 410 in a thin voice. 'No. I'm not going anywhere. I'm the . . . err . . . co-parent of this child. I am Shahenshah. I am a strong man. *Mooch nahin toh kooch nahin*.'

The doctor takes out a ten-inch-long epidural injection.

410 looks at it and faints.

'We see this every single day,' says Nurse Asha as she carries him out with the help of two assistants. 'That's why women can deliver, and men can't.'

'Ladoo,' asks the doctor. 'Are you sure you don't want an epidural? I have kept everything ready for it in case you change your mind.'

Ladoo shakes her head. No.

A nurse brings a non-stress test machine and places two belts on Ladoo's stomach.

'Press the button every time you feel a contraction,' the nurse tells Ladoo.

Ladoo does this obediently, as she nervously peers at the needle moving across the chart. After a few minutes, the doctor looks at the chart.

'Foetal heart rate is slow!' says the doctor urgently. The mood in the room changes to one of anxiety. 'We will have to monitor you closely, Ladoo. We may have to do an emergency C-section, ok?'

Ladoo looks nervously at Tamara and Bua. They pat her to calm her down.

'No, Dr Ma'am,' says Ladoo, catching her breath. 'I want a normal delivery, without an epidural or surgery. After all, my heart rate also slowed down after seeing that epidural injection!'

'Good to see that your humour is still intact,' says the doctor. 'I'll give it thirty more minutes. If you're not able to deliver by then, it will put your life, and the baby's life, in danger. I will have no option but to wheel you to the OT and do an emergency delivery, ok? Be prepared for that.'

Ladoo nods. Her eyes well up with tears. How has she come so far, to face fresh troubles?

Tamara runs out of the room and calls her mother on the phone, 'Mom, Dids' life is in danger! You have to come here. Now! Room 111. AIIMS hospital.'

Mrs Joshi comes running into the room within minutes.

'Maa?' says Ladoo in relief.

'Mom?' says Tamara, also relieved. 'How did you get here so fast?'

'Sandeep's father had a heart attack an hour ago,' says Mrs Joshi. 'I brought him to the hospital. He's in the emergency room, one floor down.'

'Where's Sandy?' asks Ladoo.

'He was in office when it happened. He just reached the hospital,' says Mrs Joshi.

'And Kavya?' asks Tamara.

'She's gone for some second honeymoon trip with her husband,' says Mrs Joshi.

Tamara and Ladoo smile at each other on hearing this.

'I'm so glad you're here, Mom,' says Tamara and hugs her mother.

'My daughter is in labour,' says Mrs Joshi. 'I cannot leave her alone. My daughter will not suffer the way I did!'

'Is Sandeep's father ok?' asks Ladoo.

'You keep quiet, beta,' says Mrs Joshi. She sits down beside Ladoo and strokes her hand gently. 'Why didn't you call me the second the contractions started? If anything happens to you or my grandchild, I'll never forgive myself.'

Ladoo gets another contraction and scrunches her face in agony. Mrs Joshi looks at Ladoo and her heart breaks. Then, an idea strikes her. She whispers something to the anaesthesiologist, who whispers something to a nurse. The nurse comes back with a trolley. The anaesthesiologist puts a mask on Ladoo's face. Ladoo resists and then suddenly starts smiling. A second later, she is giggling. Her pain is gone.

'Mom, what magic have you done?' asks Tamara incredulously.

'Nitrous oxide . . . laughing gas,' says Mrs Joshi. 'Kavya gave me this useful tip for a painless delivery!'

'You mean to say Dids is . . . *high*?' asks Tamara suspiciously.

Mrs Joshi nods mischievously. The doctor checks Ladoo.

'Amazing!' she says. 'Baby's head has dropped. Well done, Ladoo. Just two or three big pushes and your baby will be out!'

Ladoo smiles.

'Ladoo, don't smile so much. Women should look harrowed during labour, not happy. Push and pretend to be in pain. Here, have some Hajmola. The baby will slip right out like a fart,' says Mrs Joshi.

'Maa!' says Tamara in protest. 'Why are you acting like a kid?'

'Because I'm going to be a nani,' Mrs Joshi says in glee.

'My parents are tube lights,' says Tamara.

Mrs Joshi shoves a Hajmola tablet into Ladoo's mouth and takes her daughter's hand. Ladoo grunts and pushes. She sweats profusely. She almost crushes Tamara and her mother's hands.

A baby wails.

'Congratulations!' says the doctor. 'It's a healthy baby boy!'

The doctor holds up a squirming little baby. Everyone claps in joy. Ladoo stares at the baby, finding no words to express her joy, her pain forgotten. Mrs Joshi, Bua and Tamara begin to cry, as the nurses clean him up and the on-call paediatrician checks his Apgar score. When they bring him back, Ladoo holds her son against her chest. She can't stop kissing him.

She whispers in her son's ears, 'Welcome to the world, Barfi. Now I know I'll never need another man in my life. I will only love you. What fun we're going to have together!'

410 and Mr Joshi walk in. Tears roll down their cheeks when they see Barfi.

'Can I hold him?' asks Tamara.

'No, me first,' says Mrs Joshi.

'No, me first. I'm the nanu,' says Mr Joshi.

Everyone reaches out to hold the baby.

'Sterilizer! Sterilizer! Sterilizer!' shouts 410. 'No one touch my baby without cleaning your hands!'

They all laugh.

Mrs Joshi's phone beeps just then. She opens a message and her face falls.

'Is that Sandy's father?' asks Ladoo. 'Is he ok?'

Mrs Joshi takes a big gulp and says, 'Err . . . you don't worry about all that. Focus on your son.'

Just then, a nurse asks Ladoo, 'Baby name?'

Everyone looks at Ladoo. She looks at her son.

'His pet name is obviously Barfi. And his full name is Aarav Joshi. Aarav means peace, which he's brought into my life.'

'We'll ask you that after one month of no sleep,' says the doctor.

Ladoo turns to her baby—her Aarav—and laughs.

24

It's 3 a.m. A newborn baby wails. A dim light comes on in Ladoo's room.

'Dids, go back to sleep,' whispers Tamara. 'You haven't slept in two nights. I'll give Barfi your pumped milk.'

Mr and Mrs Joshi's room lights come on.

'Barfi woke up two hours ago. He cannot be hungry again!' mumbles Mrs Joshi. Then, she shouts to Ladoo, 'Beta, I'll come check his diaper.'

'I told you girls to not make Barfi sleep in the cot,' Mr Joshi says loudly. 'In our time, babies used to sleep on the bed with the parents.'

'What do you know about kids, ji?' Mrs Joshi yells. 'You've not even picked up Barfi yet!'

'I'm being careful. What if he falls from my hands?' Mr Joshi yells back.

Bua's lights come on and she shouts, 'Don't scold Bhaiya so much, Bhabhi. Poor thing! He wakes up at 5 a.m. to make tea for all of us!'

'Bua,' shouts Tamara. 'Tomorrow is my turn to bathe Barfi. You've been cheating by bathing him for two days straight!'

'Who's the one cheating by swaddling him every time?' shouts Bua.

'I took over 410's turn since he was busy, as usual, kissing Meera on the phone,' Tamara shouts back.

'Speaking of phones, Tammy,' shouts Mrs Joshi. 'Why did you tweet Barfi's potty video on Insta?'

'Maa, it's not called tweeting, but posting!' shouts Tamara. 'And can you please change your profile pic on Insta? We all know you're the anda!'

'Unlike you, I prefer to be low-key, Tammy!' shouts Mrs Joshi. 'Otherwise, who knows, the government will steal my social media data.'

'What data? All they'll find are cooking recipes and Big Boss gossip,' shouts Tamara.

'You keep quiet, Tammy!' shouts Mrs Joshi.

'Why do I feel like I'm no longer your favourite child?' shouts Tamara.

'Because I'm the favourite now!' shouts Ladoo.

'Shhh!' shouts Bua. 'You're all very loud! The whole colony will wake up!'

'You're right, Bua. Let me read Barfi a book,' says Tamara. 'That should put him to sleep.'

She opens a book titled *Progressive Rhymes and Rhythms*.

'Mickey Mouse. Good,' she says softly. 'Let's sing.'

Mickey on a railway,
Picking up stones.
Down came an engine,
And broke Mickey's bones.
Ha! said Mickey,
That's not fair.
Oh! said the engine driver,
I don't care.

Tamara shuts the book in shock.

'What is this?' she whispers to Ladoo. 'So violent! No wonder Mickey looks traumatized.'

She opens another book, *Three Little Pigs*. She reads it quickly and shuts it.

'How is this a children's book?' she says and shudders. 'Animals are being cooked alive!'

'Most children's nursery rhymes are pretty dark,' says Ladoo. '*Humpty Dumpty* is about body shaming. *Ding Dong Bell* is about a "pussy" drowned in the well. *Rock-a-Bye Baby* is about a baby falling from a treetop. *Oranges and Lemons* is about men about to have their heads chopped off. *Here We Go Round the Mulberry Bush* is about female prisoners being OCD. *London Bridge Is Falling Down* is about burying kids alive. *Three Blind Mice* makes fun of the visually impaired. You know all this, don't you?'

No, Tamara says and shakes her head. 'I can't believe I used to sing these so innocently as a six-year-old. I grew up subconsciously assimilating some pretty graphic stuff.' She pauses dramatically. 'That explains *so* much.'

'Even our *Lakdi Ki Kathi* talks about tormenting horses,' shouts Bua.

'That poor *ghoda*,' says Ladoo. 'Ok, but there are many other *nicer* nursery rhymes. Like *Jack and Jill*.'

Tamara pauses, 'But why does Jill have to come tumbling after Jack? Doesn't she have her own agency. Even that day Kavya's daughter what's-her-name . . . '

'Binny,' says Ladoo.

'Binny asked me why I was working,' says Tamara, 'because Peppa Pig's mother stays at home and only her daddy goes to work. First of all, what is a Peppa Pig? And why is all this so sexist, Dids? The mothers all stay at home and the fathers go out to work! The little girls play house-house, while the boys go out on adventures.'

'So, you're no longer a bad feminist?' asks Ladoo, unable to keep from grinning.

'No,' Tamara says, rising up on her feet. 'From now on I will be a good feminist. I will teach kids about working moms and girls who play cricket. Fathers who change diapers and boys who make sandesh. I will change books and rhymes. For example . . .'

She opens the page to another rhyme and sings:

Peter Peter pumpkin-eater,
Had a wife but couldn't keep her;
He put her in a pumpkin shell
And there he kept her very well.

'Does Peter not know that no means no?' says Tamara angrily, 'How about changing this to . . .'

Peter Peter pumpkin-eater,
Had a wife but couldn't please her;
He tried to put her in a pumpkin shell
She packed her bags and said 'go to hell'.

Tamara slams the book shut loudly. Ladoo laughs.

Tamara looks lovingly at Barfi, gurgling in the cot. 'I will not let my *laadla* grow up in a box. He will wear pink, and play with dolls, and be a dancer or chef or whatever he wants. He will be sensitive and not afraid to express his feelings. He will grow up to be a good person, not a good boy. And I will never let him listen to people saying "boys don't cry".'

On cue, Barfi starts crying.

Ladoo grins and says, 'I don't think crying will be a problem for him.'

Tamara glares at her sister.

'I knew this would happen. I knew you'd turn into a helicopter co-mom,' says Ladoo. 'It's always the bindaas ones.'

'Taking care of a newborn baby has taught me the most important lesson about having kids,' says Tamara.

Ladoo looks at her and asks, 'And what's that?'

'Don't have kids,' says Tamara. 'My earlier intuition was right. Being a mother is hard, hard work. And it's thankless. No one gives you an award for being a supermom! It's not worth it, Dids. I can't do it.'

'So, now you're going to be childless?' asks Ladoo.

'It's called child-free, Dids,' says Tamara. 'You are so *not* woke.'

'That's because I'm too busy being a-woke,' says Ladoo. 'Get it? A Woke?

'FML!' says Tamara.

'I'm asking because then I'll give away Barfi's clothes and shoes, and not save them for my future nephew or niece. I feel like he's outgrowing them every week.'

'Do it,' says Tamara. She stands up on the bed and sings, '*Kyunki . . . mujhko apni uterus se pyari hai apni azadi.*'

'Oye, oye!' says Ladoo, raising her eyebrows. 'I think the lack of sleep is making us basket cases. Sit down.'

Tamara sits down.

Ladoo takes out some books from her cupboard and lays them out on the bed.

'I knew you'd come to your senses soon enough,' she tells Tamara. 'So, I got a bunch of feminist baby books that I knew you'd love.'

Tamara eyes the books with pleasure. She runs her hands through *My First Book of Feminism (for Boys)*, *Franny's Father Is a Feminist*, *Teddy's Favorite Toy*, *Feminist Baby*, *Abba's Day* and *The Unboy Boy*. She picks up Kamla Bhasin's book of nursery rhymes called *Housework Is Everyone's Work—Rhymes for Just and Happy Families*, and reads aloud from a page:

It's Sunday, it's Sunday
Holiday and fun day.
No mad rush to get to school

No timetable, no strict rule.
Mother's home and so is the father
All of us are here together.
Father's like a busy bee
Making us cups of hot tea.
Mother sits and reads the news
Now and then she gives her views.
It's Sunday, it's Sunday
Holiday and fun day.

Tamara finishes singing and smiles, 'This is much better.'

Just then, Mrs Joshi walks into the room and picks up Barfi. She coos at him. He giggles.

'Maa, why are you here?' says Ladoo. 'And haven't I told you? No eye contact at night! Otherwise, Barfi will not go back to sleep!'

'Don't teach me parenting, you rascal,' says Mrs Joshi. 'I've raised two kids!'

'Ladoo, I'll warm up some haldi milk for you,' shouts Bua. 'It'll help you go back to sleep.'

Everyone shouts, 'No, you'll burn it!'

Kavya's house light comes on.

'Joshiyon!' shouts Kavya. 'It's past three in the morning, and you're all making so much noise. You have to Ferberize Barfi, like I'd taught. Let him cry till he falls asleep!'

'Kamini Kavya,' shouts Tamara. 'Don't give us gyan about my nephew.'

The hall light comes on, as Mrs Joshi shouts, 'Can you both stop fighting in the middle of the night, as well?

Tomorrow is Barfi's naamkaran and I can't find my havan kund. Where did I keep it?'

'Maa, this is what happens when you invite everyone at Swarg Lok!' shouts Ladoo.

'I had to show off my grandson,' Mrs Joshi shouts back.

'I don't know why you're doing a naamkaran *after* you've named him,' shouts Kavya. 'What if the priest says that Barfi's name should begin with Z?'

Barfi cries again.

'See, you even made him cry,' shouts Tamara accusingly.

Everyone, including Kavya, shouts, 'Shhh . . . shhhh . . . shhh.'

Ladoo snuggles with her baby and whispers, 'Barfi, you're the world's luckiest baby. So many people love you. They're all our Mr Rights.'

Tamara looks at another poem and reads aloud,

The clouds are gone—it's sunshine weather
Let's wash clothes along with mother
Mother will soap them
Father will wring them
And you and I
Will hang 'em to dry
When they're dry and ironed crisp
Let's dress quickly for a trip

Kavya shouts, 'I swear if she doesn't shut it . . . I'll—'

'I'll what, Kamini Kavya?' asks Tamara.

'I'll create an Insta account under the handle "Hotter Yogini" and post videos and photos of me doing asanas in a bikini. You know I have a hotter body than you do!'

Tamara opens her mouth in shock. She's about to say something back, thinks better of it, and in a sing-song voice adds, 'Ok, good night, sweet dreams! See you at the naamkaran tomorrow, you *baddest* feminist!'

25

Ladoo is in her room, trying to convince Mr Joshi to hold Barfi, when the doorbell rings.

Tamara comes running to Ladoo's room and whispers excitedly, 'Dids, you will never guess who's come!'

Ladoo looks at her sister confused.

'Shirtless—' Tamara says and looks at her father. 'I mean . . . 10 o'clock . . . '

'Sandeep?' asks Mr Joshi, with a knowing smile. 'Why's he here?'

'Who cares? The point is that he's here!' says Tamara. 'Remember, his marriage is *khalaas*, so now he's single and bindaas!'

Mr Joshi glares at Tamara and leaves.

Ladoo rolls her eyes at her sister and says, 'Let's go out before Bua serves him burnt chai.' She picks up Barfi and starts walking.

'Wait! You cannot go out looking like this,' says Tamara. 'Your kameez has milk stains. You've not combed your hair in three days. Please! This is Shirtless Sandy we are talking about!'

'New mothers look like this! Messy! Harrowed! He'll understand,' says Ladoo.

But Tamara combs Ladoo's hair. She puts a colourful dupatta on top of her kameez and forces her to wear lipstick and kajal. Only then they go out to the living room, where Bua and Mrs Joshi are clucking around an awkward Sandeep.

'Beta?' Mrs Joshi asks him. 'Will you eat motichoor ladoos?'

Bua intercepts her, 'Bhabhi, does Sandy look like he eats ladoos? See his muscles!'

Sandeep stands up on seeing Ladoo.

'Hi!' he tells Ladoo. 'I'm sorry I dropped in without calling. I don't have your number.'

'So, take her number,' says Tamara. 'It's—'

'Tammy!' warns Ladoo.

But Sandeep is distracted by Barfi, 'He's so cute! What a handsome fellow!'

'Just like you,' says Tamara.

'Tammy!' says Mrs Joshi. 'Why don't you go inside and make tea for Sandeep?'

'With ginger and a pinch of cinnamon,' says Ladoo.

'You remember?' asks Sandeep.

'I drink my tea like that now,' says Ladoo.

Sandeep flashes Ladoo a big smile. Tamara grins and says, 'BRB!'

She drags Bua with her.

Sandeep picks up a bouquet of flowers and gives it to Ladoo.

'I wanted to get a nice gift,' he says, 'but I didn't know what to buy for a baby. So, I got the mommy something.'

'Thanks,' says Ladoo. 'Lilies are my favourite.'

'Really? Mine too,' says Sandeep.

Sandeep then turns to Mr Joshi and says, 'Sir, I don't know if you know, but I refused that promotion. I don't deserve it. I told them straight that you're the best man for the job.'

'Arré beta,' says Mr Joshi. 'I also refused that post. In fact, I've taken VRS. Voluntary retirement is good for me. Both my daughters are earning well, and I want to spend time with my grandson.'

'Papa, first pick up your grandson,' Ladoo teases him.

She tries to hand Barfi to her father. He reaches out, but then retracts. Ladoo sighs.

'He is the only other man in this house,' quips Mr Joshi. 'He'll understand.'

'Sandeep,' says Mrs Joshi. 'Again, I'm sorry about your papa. He was a good man.'

'Thanks, Ma'am,' says Sandeep.

'Call me Aunty, beta,' says Mrs Joshi.

'Ok. Aunty, I never got the chance to thank you for bringing Papa to the hospital that day,' he says. He clears his throat. 'Actually, I came to talk to you all about that.'

They look at each other quizzically.

'I know this will sound like I'm crazy. But Barfi, that's his name, right?'

They all nod.

'The hospital staff told me that Barfi was born a minute after my father passed away. I know it's idiotic, but my instinct tells me that my father has been reborn—'

He stops and says, 'Sorry, I sound mad.'

'It's ok, beta,' says Mr Joshi. 'We're all mad here.'

Sandeep smiles and continues, 'I think my father has been reborn as Barfi.'

Sandeep looks at Ladoo for approval. She nods, confused.

'I know how crazy I sound, Ladoo,' he adds.

'No, beta,' says Mrs Joshi. 'This type of thinking is normal in a spiritual place like Rishikesh.'

Sandeep sighs in relief and says, 'Ok. Good to know! Anyway, I came to ask if I can drop in to see Barfi. And Billi, of course. I'm apparently a dada, thanks to her.' He chuckles awkwardly, as he looks at Billi, licking her bum. 'Once in a while only, I promise. I don't want to burden you guys.'

'Of course, beta!' says Mrs Joshi. 'Come every day if you want. After all, Barfi is your father!'

Ladoo looks down at the floor, mortified.

'Beta, I think what my Mrs means is that you can think of this as your home,' says Mr Joshi. 'There's no formality.'

Sandeep smiles and says, 'Sir, you'll laugh, but at Papa's funeral I realized that there's no one to light my pyre when I go. I'm all alone in this world.'

Just then, Tamara enters carrying a big tray of food. 'Arré, Sandy, I always say: don't take tension, always give tension. You are not alone. Think of our Barfi as your Barfi, of our house as your house, of our Ladoo as your Ladoo.'

'Tammy!' warns Ladoo.

'First Varun . . . then 410 . . . now Sandy!' Bua mumbles under her breath. 'Ladoo was looking for one father and now thousands are dropping from the sky!'

Sandeep laughs and says, 'You're very lucky, Ladoo.'

'I know,' says Ladoo and smiles.

Just then Mr Joshi takes Barfi in his hands.

'Papa, you did it! You picked Barfi up!' says Ladoo. 'Jai Bholenath!'

They all gather around Mr Joshi in excitement.

Barfi gurgles. Sandeep reaches out to touch him.

Everyone shouts together, 'Sterilizer!'

Acknowledgements

I'd like to begin by thanking the benevolent moron who told me I'd be redundant for five years after having children. It was her arrogation that pushed me to be at my most productive, in what I call the 'udder phase' of my life—four years, two babies, four published books, two movie scripts, podcasts, shows, articles, TV debates, speeches, lit fests, and terrible WhatsApp manners. Motherhood gave me wings. It didn't clip them.

I want to thank my many (unnamed) friends, who put themselves through hell and back to have a biological child. From freezing embryos, to performing IUI or IVF, doing uterine biopsies, realigning uterine linings, going through countless injections, medications, procedures and tests, you did not stop till you heard that slushy sound of your baby's heartbeat. Your story and candour, which you so generously shared with me, helped me capture Ladoo's grief of what she perceived as her empty womb and the failure of her body. Thank you for showing us that our ovaries don't have an expiration date, only our mindset does.

I'd like to thank the rigours of pregnancy: the severe nausea that once made me lose my voice for ten days. The haemorrhoids that seemed to be having their own sympathetic pregnancy. My labour pains that sawed my body into half. The cold plunge into motherhood, with sleeplessness so severe, that a long blink would feel like a nap. Because being a mother was all it took, for me to *really* respect the foresight of my friends who decided *not* to have children. Lying sloth-like and Victorianesque, googling the ill-effects of liposuction to talk myself out of it, was a good counterpoint to liking photos of my child-free friends dancing in the Masai Mara and featuring in *40 under 40* lists. You giving me FOMO is the reason I'm not completely consumed by motherhood and work the way I do.

Which reminds me—thank you to all those taunts you threw my way, you know who you are, for not having kids early in life. Having kids early gave you bragging rights. Having them late gave me a story.

Thank you to the pandemic, our unexpected visitor that overstayed its welcome so much, it may be Indian, not Chinese. You converted me into a banana-bread-baking bank-robber-lookalike, wallowing in such gloom, that I was left too exhausted to write anything but comedy. Weary of seeing strong and powerful women portrayed as crazy, screechy, vampy bitches in our movies, I wrote Ladoo's character to show that a strong and powerful woman is usually just a normal, regular and even *funny* family gal.

I'd like to thank Sidharth Jain, founder of The Story Ink and a champion for writers, for seeing the value in Ladoo's story, and guiding me on how to put it to screen. Thanks to you, the book will soon be seen as a major motion picture, with a mega studio to boot!

I'd like to thank the wonderful team at Penguin Random House India, who have published many of my books, and published them well. Gurveen Chadha, my editor, who so passionately and quickly picked up my book and brought it out. The lovely Milee Ashwarya, who started out as my publisher, and became a friend; with whom I share a love for our little girls. Shruti Katoch, Sonjuhi Negi, Saloni Mital, Rachna Pratap, Lisamma Kuriakose and cover designer Akangksha Sarmah, who've helped to bring this book so beautifully together.

As always, this book is ultimately dedicated to my family. My two real-life ladoos: my three-year-old daughter Amara, whose name inspires my novels, and my nine-month-old daughter Aria, whose name was inspired by novels. Your names mean 'eternal' and 'noble' respectively, and you're both truly my eternal nobility—except for what you did to my bladder.

My wonderful husband Sahil Kanuga, whom I'm always tempted to ask, 'What's it like being married to a ghost?' You must be mad for enduring me when I'm submerged in my writing—physically present but mentally absent—and yet always being proud of everything I do, even if it's making a simple cup of chai (with adrak and a dash of cinnamon).

To my mother, Sujata Pant, for being an indulgent Nani, something we never expected of a gold medallist from Punjab University and the Chief Commissioner (retired) of Income Tax. Thanks for teaching me that '*show me a working woman without guilt, and I'll show you a man*' never applied to our family, so I could use that against you, by moving into your building, and making you babysit my kids, while I wrote.

I hope you enjoy *The Terrible, Horrible, Very Bad Good News*. This book is special for several reasons. It's the fourth book I wrote as a new mother—after *Feminist Rani, How To Get Published in India* and *The Holy* 100. It's the first in my 'books for movies' series i.e. books written specifically for screen, and will soon hit your nearest movie theatre under the name *Badnam Ladoo*. It's also my first attempt at writing humour, and hopefully not my last—if you show the book some love, especially on Amazon, and refrain from asking for free copies. Happy reading!